My Cowboy
Emma & Cade

BROOKE MAY

My Cowboy
Copyright 2015 Brooke May
Edited by Editing4Indies
Cover by Dark Water Covers

This book is a work of fiction. Names, characters, places, and incidents are the product of the author's imagination or are used fictitiously. Any resemblance to actual events, locales, or person, living or dead, is coincidental.

All Rights Reserved. In accordance with the U.S. Copyright Act of 1976, the scanning, and electronic sharing of any part of this book without the permission of the publisher or author constitute piracy and theft of the author's intellectual property. If you would like to use material from this book (other than for review purpose), prior written permission must be obtained by contacting the publisher at *bmay3129@gmail.com* . Thank you for your support of the author's rights.

FBI Anti-Piracy Warning: The unauthorized reproduction of distribution of a copyrighted work is illegal. Criminal copyright infringement, including infringement with monetary gain, in investigated by the FBI and is punishable by up to five years in federal prison and a fine of $250,000.

To my Family and close friends that were there for me and believed in me and my dreams

Prologue

"COME ON, CADE!" Libby and I cheer as Cade takes his last ride for the high school rodeo finals.

"Get 'em, you fucker!" I take a quick glance at my big brother hanging over the railing yelling at his best friend.

I roll my eyes and turn back to Cade and the bull. The buzzer sounds and Cade makes his move to dismount, successfully landing on two feet. The crowd cheers as he waves around before going to get his rope.

"Damn! That boy of mine is pretty amazing." I turn around to see my dad, Frank, and Cade's dad, Nathan, walk up to us. My dad nods in agreement as he takes a drag from his nasty cigarette.

"Do you have to smoke that, Dad?" Tucker glares over at our father. The only reason that he's pissed is because he can't smoke right now. My dad takes the cigarette out, looks at it, flicks it to the ground, and stomps it out. "Thank you," Tucker says with a stiff jaw.

I look around and see that the crowd has died down over the last couple of days. This is the final day of events for the high school final then tonight is the award ceremony.

When I look back toward the arena, I see Cade making his way back to us. He is carrying his rope and wearing a big handsome smile. I didn't hear his score, but it must have been good.

I run up to him and give him a quick hug. "Great ride, Cade!" I smile up at him. He's freakishly tall, but then again, I haven't reached my full height, yet.

"Thanks, monster." He pats me on the shoulder and moves on to the men.

"Monster, still?" I turn to look at Libby, who is grinning. We have been best friends since we were little, just like our mothers before us.

I let out a sigh and start walking with her to our horse trailer. "I'll never be more than his best friend's kid sister."

"Well, duh...we are four years younger than both of them." Libby glances over her shoulder at my brother. Where as my crush on Cade goes unnoticed, Libby openly admits to having one on my brother. Tucker ignores it; he doesn't see her as anything but a little sister.

"I think I should find a boy our age who would get my mind off of him." I look down. There is no boy our age who I like. Fourteen-year-old boys are still little kids; I want an older boy who has grown up.

"Me, too." Libby sighs. "I'm ready to go home."

"I agree. I hate the award ceremony. I'm glad this is Tucker and Cade's last year in high school rodeo." I look around for my mom and Rebecca, Libby's mom, so we can start home ahead of our dads and the boys.

"Yeah. Has Tucker said anything about what he plans on doing now that they've graduated?" She's fishing for answers to see if he will be around a little longer.

"Army." Her shock shows through her eyes plain as day, but she quickly recovers.

"Oh."

"He wants to join." I love my brother but I worry about everything that is going on in the world today and what might happen to him. "I'm just glad that he couldn't talk Cade into going with him." I thank God for that. They fight about it all the time. Cade supports my brother, but he doesn't want that type of life

My Cowboy

"What does Cade plan on doing?" Libby quickly questions me as we see our moms make their way toward us.

"Pro Rodeo Circuit," I say sadly. I was hoping that he would stay close for college, but he doesn't plan on going. Instead, he wants to follow in his dad's footsteps and compete in rodeos for a few years. I'm happy for him, but I'll miss him.

"You girls ready to head home?" I look up at my mom, which isn't far; she's really short.

"Yes, Mom, we're ready." I smile and walk toward her car.

"Margaret, I'm running to the restroom real quick then we can hit the road," Rebecca says as she walks off. My mom simply nods. Libby and I glance at each other and let out a little laugh. Rebecca isn't going to use the restroom; she's going to say good-bye to Nathan. She's been after him for years, ever since his wife left him and Cade. But Nathan doesn't feel the same; he hasn't had a relationship in as long as I can remember.

Once we have Casper behind us, an uneasy feeling comes over me. I brush it off not quite sure what it means but feel like something bad is going to happen. Every time I get this feeling, something always happens. Once I was at school and this feeling came over me, I rushed down to the office and called home to make sure everyone was okay. Turned out my dad broke his arm when one of the horses he was breaking in had thrown him off.

I look over at Libby and whisper, "Something bad is coming."

Her eyes go wide; she's one of my believers, as well as our moms. My dad and brother, not so much. "What?"

"Not sure."

~*~*~*~

THE HIGHWAY FLIES by, and four hours later, we are back home in the little ranch town of Elk Field, in Wyoming. We drop Libby and Rebecca off in town and then head out to our family ranch.

Once home, I set about doing all my chores that have fallen behind, which mainly consist of taking care of my horse, Gema. She's been out in the pasture all week; I'm going to need to run her. Before I get the chance to take her out, my mom comes running out of the house. I watch as she rushes up to me, and then I see the tears. *No, something did happen.* "Mom?"

"Oh, God, Emma! We need to go!" She grabs my hand that was holding Gema's reins.

"Mom, I need to put Gema away then."

"No time!" She rushes us over to her car and urges me in. *What is going on?*

"Mom?" I question her as she starts the car and peels out of the driveway. "What's going on? You're scaring me."

"Oh, sweetheart." She's crying now. "There was an accident. Nate and..." She starts crying heavily.

"Not Dad." I stare at her with wide eyes. I'm trying to keep the tears contained. They rode down together following Cade and Tucker.

She shakes her head. "No...Cade." I blanch. No! No! No! Not Cade. I start crying as well. *Please don't let him be gone.*

"W...wh...what about Cade?" I'm crying so heavily that I can barely understand myself.

"He was riding back with Nate and their truck rolled." She grips the steering wheel tightly until her knuckles turn white. "Cade is being rushed to the nearest hospital. I....I don't know 'bout Nate," she says weakly. I simply nod.

~*~*~*~

WE ARRIVE BACK in Casper and rush to the hospital. Once there, we make our way to the waiting room to find my dad and brother. I rush over to Tucker and grab him in for a hug. "Cade?" I whisper into his shoulder.

"I don't know yet. They've had him back there for a while now." Tucker pulls me into a tight embrace. I start to cry into his shoulder, hysterically balling my eyes out. I love Cade. Yeah, I'm still a little girl, but I've loved him since I started to notice boys. I dream about the day that he will notice me, when I'm older, of course. I can't imagine a future in this world without him in it.

I look up at my parents; my dad is quietly consoling my mom. "Nate?" she cries out. My dad looks down at her tiny frame and shakes his head. She steps back, shaking her head in disbelief. "No. No. No!" She turns to start pacing, but my dad pulls her back into his arms.

I turn back to my brother and look into his eyes. "He didn't make it, Em." I've never heard Tucker sound so defeated. "They pronounced him dead at the scene." I fall to my knees, bury my face in my hands, and start to cry uncontrollably.

"Cade Masters?" We all look up to see a doctor standing there with a clipboard.

"Is he okay?" My dad steps up.

"Are you his father?" The doctor glances up from the board.

My dad shakes his head. "No, but we are all he has left." He gestures to the three of us that now stand behind him.

The doctor nods. "He'll be fine. His leg had a piece of the vehicle lodged into it. He lost quite a bit of blood, but he will be fine." He moves out of our way. "He's awake if you would like to go back and see him."

My dad nods as he takes both my mom and my hands and leads us down the hall.

I freeze at the door. Seeing Cade lying in the bed all bruised up and hurt break my heart. I stay back and quiet as my parents and brother talk to him.

"Hey, monster." I look up through my tears at him. He's giving me a weak smile. "You're too tough for tears." I nod my head and look back down to try to stop the tears.

"Do you remember anything, Cade?"

He shakes his head then winces. "Careful, Cade." My mom is hovering over him.

"Pop and I were joking around, and the next thing I knew, the truck was rolling." He looks at all of us. "I don't remember anything after the first roll." He looks down at his legs that are covered by blankets. "I can't believe he's gone," he says quietly.

I push past my parents and give him a careful hug. He lifts his hand that is free of an IV and his head to rest on my shoulder in attempt to hug me back. "I'm glad you're okay, Cade. I'm so sorry for your dad." I try not to cry again, but it's hard.

I feel one of his hands hold my head to his shoulder. "Thanks, Emma." I give a weak smile that no one can see. In the rare moments that he says my name, it brightens me up.

I step back and into my mom's arms. "We are here for you, Cade. You are family," my dad states as he places a hand on Cade's shoulder and lightly squeezes.

He simply nods. "You guys go get something to eat. I'll be fine," he says weakly not looking at any of us.

As much as I don't want to leave him alone, we do. I'm the last one out the door and I hear him. "What the hell do I do now?" I chance a peek at him, seeing his head fall back against the pillow with his eyes closed.

"You survive, Cade," I whisper, not sure if he can hear me. I shut the door and follow my family back down the hallway.

~*~*~*~

I'M EXCITED ABOUT today. A week has passed since the accident, and today Cade comes home. My mom has been busy arranging Nate's funeral with Rebecca while my dad has been trying to find ways for Cade busy to keep busy and not sink further into depression.

I have a little skip in my step as I walk down the hallway to his room with my dad and brother. Tucker tried again to talk Cade into going into the Army with him, but it pissed Cade off so much that he told Tucker to leave. I've never seen them yell at each other like that before.

My dad opens Cade's door and freezes. He turns to me and Tucker with a frown in place then grabs a nurse who is hurrying by. "Excuse me, miss." The nurse looks up at him. "Do you know where Cade Masters is?"

What? He's not in there? I push past Tucker and look into a now clean and empty room. *Where would he go?*

"Yes sir, he checked out about two hours ago." The nurse continues on her way. *Checked out? Why would he leave without us?*

I look questionably up at Tucker, who is now pissed. "That dipshit." He punches the wall and storms back down the hallway.

I turn to my dad. "Where is he, Dad?"

Shaking his head, he grabs my hand and follows Tucker. "He'll be back, Emma." He gives me an encouraging smile. "He'll be back."

Chapter One

<u>10 Years Later...</u>

I WILL NOT CRY. I will not cry. I will not cry, I repeat to myself as I drive out to the ranch. What has become of my life in the last eight months? Shit, that's what. Well, actually, if I think about it, it's been going downhill for the past couple of years, starting with Tucker.

Tucker joined the Army right after Cade disappeared. He was so pissed that his best friend left like that, he wanted to get away as soon as he could. He made it through three tours in Iraq and Afghanistan and was well into his fourth tour when a roadside bomb hit his truck. Tucker survived, but he hasn't been the same since. He lost his left leg, and it scarred him badly.

He had planned on coming home and taking over the ranch for my dad after his fourth tour. Now, he just sits in the living room pissed all the time. His physical therapy has helped, and he gets around well with his prosthetic leg, but he can't ride a horse anymore.

He broke up with his girlfriend; they were completely in love with each other. Maddi gave up everything to move out here while Tucker was healing. She is an amazing person and a great friend to Libby and me. She stayed here after the break-up and moved in with Libby and her mom. I hope that she and Tucker can work everything out. My brother is a dumbass, but he can't really help it right now with his PTSD.

The one smart thing that he did was force me to stay in college instead of dropping out to help our dad on the ranch since

My Cowboy

he couldn't do much. Now, I really need my ranch management degree more than anything. Why? My dad, Franklin Hunter Price, passed away three months ago. He didn't get to see me graduate, bring the ranch back, or meet his grandchildren.

Mom has her good days, but lately, most are bad. I try to do what I can for both her and Tucker. I work hard on the ranch, focus on getting good grades to graduate, and work part-time at Hank's, the local cowboy bar.

Well, now I'm graduating in three days with my degree and plan on getting the ranch back on its feet. So, life has been hard for my family. It's been shit. We have nothing but bad luck anymore. And to top it off, my boyfriend of five years broke up with me last night while I was at work. Not that I'm upset about it I was about to do the same to him. We weren't going anywhere, but what upset me most is that the fat bastard known as Trey Barker was cheating on me with the town whore, Lilly Widiner. Wide Lilly, as Libby and I call her.

Her smug attitude was evident as she draped herself over Trey's shoulder at Hank's Bar while he broke up with me. I lost my temper, pissing Hank off. I flew over the bar, nailed her in the nose, and kicked Trey in the balls so hard that I think they started to bleed.

I have developed quite the temper, mainly because it seems everyone is always trying to tell me what to do. I want my own life and now I can have it on the ranch. Tucker can now look the other way and get his shit figured out and all mom has to focus on is her own healing. I can be left in peace.

So, why am I trying not to cry? Well, simple. The ranch is deep in the red, and I need to figure out how to fix it.

"Hey!" I shake my head and glance over to the passenger side of my truck. "Snap out of it! We already lost Tucker to all this depression shit. We don't need you to go down that road, too," Libby snaps at me. I let out a puff of air and shake my head.

"If it wasn't for you, I'm sure I would have by now." That's true. Libby has been there for me every step of the way. She even backed me up last night by taking a swing at Lilly as well.

"Good. Because life would suck without my best bitch." She is so endearing.

"Love you, too," I say dryly. "Do you think the ranch will be okay?"

She looks over and then slaps me. "Get over it! God, you're driving me nuts. I know, I know, the ranch is really important to you but focus on your stupid brother." She looks back out the window. Libby's crush on Tucker quickly died out after he joined the Army.

"Okay," I whisper even though I disagree with her. Tucker has to work out his own stuff. He still sees Maddi every other day when he goes into the diner, and I think he does it to check on her. To make sure no other guy steals her away.

We reach the ranch in no time. After I pull in front of the house, I sit there frozen staring at the two-story log house that had been my home until eight months ago. I wanted to stay out here, but Mom forced all of us to my grandma's old rental house, so Dad was closer to the hospital.

Libby's heavy sigh brings me back to myself. Stampede and Ripper, the offspring of my horse, Gema, are still out here with most of the horses and cattle. Well, the ones not currently on the mountain. I come out here every day to be with them. Along with one of my bulls, Roundhouse, and my new lab puppy, Timber, they are my own little family, my babies, and my escape.

I climb out of my old truck and wipe the sweat off my hands. "I'm headin' into the pisser, meet ya at the barn, chica." Libby hops up the steps to the wraparound deck and disappears into the house.

My Cowboy

I turn and walk toward the barn with Timber falling into step next to me. I left the boys in the barn last night mainly to keep them away from some of the mares in one of the pastures.

I stop in my tracks and tilt my head to the side. "What in the hell?" I mutter while I stare at a big black Dodge with Texas plates parked next to the barn. I hadn't noticed it when I pulled in. I look down at Timber. "Shall we see who is poking their nose around here, girl?" She yips and wags her tail. "Whoa, down you evil girl." I laugh at her as I start to walk toward the barn again.

The barn door is opened just a tiny bit, so I stop and listen for anything. I hear some stuff moving around then I hear the telltale sign of Stampede stomping his hooves. I go to grab the handle when the door flies open right into my face, knocking me back on my ass.

"Fucker! God-damn son-of-a-bitch!" I try to sit up, but damn, my head hurts so bad that I can't see. I hear Timber yipping her little heart out. Yep, she is going to be harmless. After all, she's only four months old. "Timber, will you stop!" I manage to sit up and start to rub my head.

"Jesus!" A deep, smooth voice comes from above me. I try to look up, but all I see is the outline of someone who is very tall and very buff. "I'm sorry, miss." My hand stills on the top of my head then slowly lowers to the ground as I try to get up.

"I'm fine." I stumble to get up and almost fall back down when two hands wrap around my waist. "Or not," I whisper. There is a jolt of electricity that shoots right through me the second this guy touches me.

"Man, you're a tiny little thing." The voice has some amusement to it. With his hands on me and a voice as deep and sexy as his, I'm unable to think, which adds to my headache as Timber continues to bark.

"Oh...my...God!" Libby has joined the party. I manage to stabilize myself while holding onto his arms, which are massive. I close my eyes and then slowly open them.

Everything comes back to me, and I am looking right into a massive chest that is rising and falling slowly and steadily. *Hello, muscles.* I slowly work my way up to a strong, stubble-covered jaw and a grin in place. The guy is tan, and his teeth aren't perfectly white, but that's fine. I continue my journey up till I meet his eyes. I suck in a breath and stare back in shock at the most beautiful dark chocolate brown eyes that are also smiling down at me. *I know these eyes.*

"Cade..." I whisper and feel my chest tighten up.

He hasn't let go of me, but his smile falters just the smallest bit; he looks excited. "Have we met, sugar?"

Sugar? Oh, thank God! I'm not monster anymore! I quickly step out of his hold needing the space to think. I turn and look at Libby, who is standing there dumbstruck as Timber runs circles around her. I give her a pleading look, and she regains herself.

"You got to be fuckin' shittin' me!" She walks with control up to us.

Cade lets out a laugh. Oh, that laugh, how I've missed it. It melts something deep inside me. I turn back to him. Now that a few feet separate us, I can talk. "What are you doing here?"

He removes his black Stetson and runs a hand through his dark brown hair. "Well, I use to live here, sugar. You Tucker Price's wife or something?" He puts his hat back on and pulls it lower over his eyes making him look dark and dangerous.

I arch a brow and move my hands to my hips. "I am NOT Tucker Price's wife. If that dumbass would pull his head out of his ass, he has an amazing girl waiting for him at Martha's Diner in town."

Libby is now standing next to me. "You got to be fuckin' shittin' me," she repeats a bit calmer this time. She throws her arms over her chest crossing them.

Now that we are standing next to each other Cade takes a good look passing back and forth between us. "Runt?" He looks at Libby then turns to me. "Monster?" He is shocked. He shakes his head. "No way," he says under his breath.

Libby starts to laugh. "Yep, it's us, shithead!" She moves past him and into the barn where she continues to laugh.

Cade continues to stand there staring at me in shock. I shake my head and follow Libby's lead. Once I'm alongside Cade, I stop and look up at him. "I'm not monster anymore," I whisper and walk into the barn to start saddling up Ripper as Libby saddles Stampede.

I stop in front of Ripper's stall and stare at him. He looks cleaned up. I mean, I brushed him down yesterday, but he's usually covered in straw the next morning. I look over at Stampede and notice that he, too, was cleaned up. Libby stares quizzically at him with a brush in her hand.

"What the..."

"I groomed them." Libby and I turned to look at Cade standing with his hands in his pockets at the door. "I was waiting for someone to show up." He shrugs as he moves toward us.

I look at Libby, who rolls her eyes and heads to the tack room for a saddle. I turn back to Ripper and open his stall. "Hey, boy." I pet his nose and turn to lead him out.

"Hard to believe it's been ten years, right, monster?" Cade is leaning against the stall gate watching me closely. *Monster again...seriously?*

I roll my eyes and push past him. "Yeah, I guess." I set to work on getting Ripper ready for his ride while Libby does the same with Stampede. "Lib, how's your jaw today?" I want to talk about something that isn't related to Cade. He left our family without a word, which upset me greatly. I moved on from him, though...I think. And after what Trey pulled, I don't need a man, especially while dealing with the drama of Tucker.

"No better than your hand." She checks to see if the saddle is cinched down tight enough then turns to me. "A little sore." She grins. "But probably not as bad as Lilly feels." She winks and gets up on Stampede.

"What did you two do to Lilly Widiner?" Cade comes up between us looking pissed and really hot.

I get up on Ripper. "Why would you care?" I lean forward in the saddle to adjust my seat and shrug. "She pissed me off, so I knocked her out." Libby clears her throat. "With Libby's help."

Cade glares up at me, but before he could speak, Libby stepped in. "She's a whore now, Cade." She kicks Stampede's sides and starts to move. "A lot has changed since you were last here. Especially Emma."

I glance down at him and give him a bittersweet smile. "Head to my grandma's in town." I kick Ripper's sides and follow Libby. "That's where you will find everyone," I call over my shoulder, leaving sexy, grown-up Cade standing at the barn door.

Chapter Two

"That boy sure got hot, didn't he?" Libby chances a glance at me, but already knows that he affected me. "I think my thong exploded," she states as she looks back out in front of us.

I throw my head down and sigh. "Oh, Lib."

"What? I haven't gotten any lately, thank you very much, and neither have you." I give her a blank stare and urge Ripper to go faster. "Well, at least I'll use my vibrator to make me happy. You, my dear, need to invest in one. Best money I've ever spent."

"So I've been told." Ten years, it really has been that long. He was cute before he left, but now, now he is insanely hot. Gone are the boyish looks, replaced with a dark, rough outdoorsmen look that suits him really well. And yet, my heart still picks up when I look into his eyes, which have hardened. "Do you bug Maddi with all the sex talk, too?"

"Well, duh! You two are my girls. I have to make up for what you two lack in the sex department."

"So you choose to be perverted," I mutter to myself.

"Like I need to answer that! You've known that since we were in high school when I got busy with Kyle Logan in the bathroom of the shop room during lunch." Yes, she is very proud of that. The school suspended her for three weeks because of it. "I need to dirty your mind up, chica."

I shake my head and let out a small laugh. "Whatever you say."

"So, Cade..."

"What about him?" I glare over at her.

She shrugs. "I'll take him if you don't want him anymore."

"Libby Nicole!" I glare over at her.

With a shit-eating grin in place, she exclaims, "I knew it! You still have the hots for him, even after all this time."

"Do not." I look out to see if I can see my beautiful Black Angus bull somewhere.

"Do, too. Just give it up. I know you too well to be lied to."

"Libby." I sigh. "It was long ago. I grew up and got over that stupid crush I had on him." *Bullshit.*

"Bullshit! I saw the way you stared at him after you got a good look. Can't say that I blame you, that boy grew up well." She winks at me again.

"Whatever. I just want to check on my bull then head home." I kick Ripper into a full-out run, leaving Libby in the dust.

~*~*~*~

WHEN WE RETURN to the barn, I am thankful that Cade is gone. But that means he is most likely at the house in town.

After we cool down the boys and let them out in the small arena to the side of the barn, we head for home. Timber curls up next to me and sleeps the whole ride. She's one tired pup from all the running that she did today.

I take Libby home first, not wanting to have her at the showdown that is more than likely happening at my house. "Call me later. I want to know everything." She rubs Timber's back then jumps out.

I watch her go up to the house and wave at Maddi, who is walking out the door. She gives me a quick wave then turns to talk to Libby.

"Well, pup, ready to head home?" Timber lazily glances up at me and yawns. I smile at her as I throw the truck in reverse and head for home.

Sure as shit, Cade's truck is parked in front of the house in my usual spot. I have to go around the block and park across the street. My truck isn't allowed in the driveway because it tends to leak oil.

I pick up Timber and carry her toward the house. She is still out, even in my arms. I wore her out good today. "Momma, I'm home!" I shout as I kick off my boots and head for the stairs to wash up.

"Okay, sweetie. Dinner is almost done," she calls from the kitchen down the hallway.

"Come on, baby girl." I rub and kiss the top of Timber's head as we climb the stairs. Once in my room, I lay her on the bed and head for the bathroom that I, unfortunately, share with my brother. We always keep the door closed so Timber and Bugle can't get into the toilets, so I think nothing of knocking when I walk in. I heard Tucker downstairs talking; I just assumed it was with Cade.

I open the door and look up to see a very naked, very hot Cade stepping out of the shower. My eyes go wide, and I am unable to move. *Holy shit!*

"Fuck!" he yells as he quickly throws the towel around him. "Jesus, Emma! Do you know how to knock?" He glares at me but doesn't shake me. I stand there with one hand on the doorknob and my phone in the other, just staring.

"Hey, monster? You in there?" I blink and shake my head looking around at anything but Cade.

"Sorry," I mumble as I step back and shut the door. I don't stop till I reach my room and slam the door shut, sinking to the floor. "Shit!" I yell quietly.

My God, though, he's hot. His build is tall, which I always knew, but his muscles are everywhere! That's one thing I really am drawn to a guy with muscles. He has a lean waist with a damn V. Oh my goody aunt, how in the hell am I going to get that image out of my head?

I throw my head back against my door and close my eyes. *Nice deep breaths.* I slowly inhale and exhale. I'll be fine. Nothing changes; he's still an ass for leaving our family.

I move to get up and set about changing my clothes for work. Throwing on a pair of clean jeans and my white tank top that has Hank's Bar across the front of it, I quickly throw my hair up in a messy bun and decide to face the music downstairs.

I fly down the stairs and into the kitchen. "Hey, Momma." I make my way to the cabinet to set the table.

"Four places tonight, sweetie." She smiles over at me. Wow, I haven't seen that smile in a while. I nod and set to work. "Cade said that he saw you out at the ranch."

"Yeah." I focus on the plates and the silverware rather than my mom's question. I stop and look up at her. She's staring at me. "What?" I frown.

"He also said you weren't very nice, Emma."

"So what?" I grab the salt and pepper to place on the table. "Does he really deserve my kindness? He left our family without a word and now he thinks he can just come right back in like nothing changed?" I slam the butter down on the table as well as the steak sauce.

"Emma Jo, that boy lost everything." She fists her hands on her hips and shoots daggers at me.

"Whatever, Mom, I'm not talking about it." I shrug and drop my hands to my sides. "I don't care." I turn to the fridge and grab the jug of tea to place on the table, too. "I'll get Tucker."

When I enter the living room, I stop at the door in shock to see a smile on Tucker's face and a laugh coming out of him. I bite my lip to contain my joy. This is the most animated I've seen him in at least a year.

I turn to see Cade talking to him; I'm not really paying attention to what they are saying. My head fills with the image of Cade's bare chest covered with water drops and my eyes go wide.

My Cowboy

I stand there staring at Cade until they both turn their attention to me. "Huh?" I shake my head noticing that Tucker asked me something.

"Is dinner done?" I turn back to my brother, who is glaring at me. I glare back and nod.

"Yes." I turn back around and storm down to the kitchen.

~*~*~*~

IT'S BEEN A while since our table has been full. I usually it across from Tucker, but he has taken my dad's spot tonight, leaving me across from Cade. All I can do is glare.

"What in the hell is your deal tonight, Emma?" I look at Tucker and shrug.

"Guess I'm just confused as to why we matter now."

Silverware either drops to plates or freezes heading toward a mouth. "Emma Jo," my mom once again scolds me.

I continue to eat, ignoring the lot of them. "So...tell me, Cade?" I look up at him. "Tired of being a rodeo cowboy, you decide to come back here hoping to be a real one again."

My mom lets out a heavy sigh while Tucker pinches the bridge of his nose and shakes his head.

Oh, we all knew what became of Cade two years after he left. By then I was so pissed that I didn't bother to keep track of him. Dad and Tucker did, though, but eventually when he didn't come back at all, Tucker gave up as well.

After he doesn't answer, I turn to my mom. "I'm moving back out to the ranch tomorrow." I take a drink of my tea. "Libby and I are going to finish moving everything out."

"Well, I guess I could use the company." I shoot a look of shock up at Cade.

"Company?" I arch a brow and wait for his answer.

"Yeah, I'm going to be taking care of things out there from now on. When I was out there, I got a good look at things that needed to get done."

I glare at him. "Fine, but understand this. You will be helping me." I turn back to my mom. "I'll take the master bedroom then." I give Cade an evil grin. "That way I can have my own private bathroom." He glares at me; I smile and turn back to my mom again. "May I be excused? I need to head to work." She simply nods. I dump my plate, rinse it off, and place it in the dishwasher. I give my mom a kiss on the cheek, as I do every time I leave. "Let Timber out in about an hour, and she'll be hungry by then. Love you."

I head for the front door when Tucker speaks up. "I'll be checking in on you later, Emma. Behave tonight. No fights."

I wave over my shoulder. "Whatever you say, big brother." I pull my boots on, grab my keys, and fly out the door.

~*~*~*~

I GLARE OVER at one of the tables in the corner where my brother and Cade sit watching me and this douche-bag who won't leave me alone. Well, Cade is watching me; Tucker is basically shooting daggers at the guy Maddi is here with. I know it is a pity date; she won't give up on Tucker.

"Come on, babe. Just one dance," he begs again.

I let out a frustrated sigh and drop my rag on the counter. "No, I'm working."

He gives me a crooked grin that makes my skin crawl. "Babe, who cares? It's slow in here. Your boss won't mind."

"Just give up, kid, before she knocks you on your ass," the man next to him mutters.

"This sweet thing lady?" He looks back at me. "I don't think so."

Ha! Obviously, he isn't a local. I smile sweetly at him and lean forward. "I would back off if I were you." I turn a quick gaze at Tucker and Cade. "See those two in the corner?" He turns to see them glaring at him. "One is my brother and he is ex-Army. He'll kick your ass after I kick it. Now," I turn to a group of girls who are here celebrating their friend's twenty-first birthday, "those girls over there are looking for fun. Go bug them." I turn back to my rag and clean the counter.

Finally, he gets up and makes his way over to the group of girls. I turn back to the man who was next to him. "You here to make sure that I don't get into another fight?" I move to refill his drink.

He grins and laughs. "No, I need something to do since your mother has stolen my wife once again."

"Where are Mom and Rebecca tonight?" Ever since Dad died, Mom and Rebecca have been spending a lot of time together. Kind of like when Jackson, Rebecca's first husband and Libby's dad, passed away when we were little.

"Movies; some chick flick they wanted to see." He takes a drink. "I'm really starting to miss my wife, Emma."

I laugh. "Yeah, Dad went through the same thing. Don't worry, Mom will be back to her old self soon, and you'll have Rebecca driving you crazy again."

"Ha!" He slaps the counter. "I am glad that you didn't punch him, though. Hate to arrest you for assault on my night off."

"Yeah, well." I wipe some water rings off the counter. "Since Tucker is here, I don't want him to get into a fight and possibly hurt himself."

He nods. "You're a good sister, Emma. A lot of people would have given up on him a long time ago."

"He can't help it; I pray someday soon he will be back to his normal self." I give him a quick smile and head down to a couple at the other end of the bar.

When I come back, Cade is leaning against the bar talking to Lee. "Can I help you?" I try to say in the nicest tone I have, but I fail.

"Glad you're back, Cade." Lee slaps his shoulder and goes to get up. He hands me enough to cover his bill. "See ya, Emma."

I smile and nod. "Sheriff."

He laughs as he heads out the door.

"How did he become sheriff?" I turn back to Cade and offer nothing but a shrug. "Another beer, please." He is following my every move.

I huff. "How much has he had to drink?"

"About six or seven."

"What?" I look past Cade to Tucker still glaring at Maddi's date. I shake my head. "You're cut off, Tucker!"

"Fuck off, Emma! I'll drink however much I want!" he yells back at me but still hasn't turned his head.

"Cade, take him home now." I slam the bar with my towel.

"Oh, get over it, Emma. He's fine." He grins at me.

I shoot a glare up at him. "You have got to be kidding me! Cade, he has PTSD, and he gets really bad when he drinks. Take him home now!" I essentially yell at him.

Before he could speak, I see Maddi shoot past us running toward the bathroom. I look at her date, who is confused and then to my brother, who is still glaring. I'm tired of this. I look back up at Cade. "Take him home now. Please. Don't stop at the liquor store or anything. Take him home and put him to bed." I move from behind the bar to make my way after Maddi. "Go home and go to bed, Tucker!" I yell as I take off down the hallway.

"Fuck you, Emma!" Tucker yells after me.

I try the door to the ladies' room and find it unlocked. "Maddi?" I slowly push it open just in case she doesn't want to talk. I hear her crying. "Maddi, want me to come in?"

"It's fine, Emma." I turn to see her sitting on the chair we keep in here; she's trying to wipe her tears. I kneel in front of her. "I did this to him, Emma. If I had just told Bobby no, everything would be fine." She starts to cry again.

"No, Tucker needs to get back on his meds and start seeing the therapist again." I wipe her tears and pull her into a hug.

My Cowboy

"I want him back, Emma." She bawls into my shoulder. "I miss him so much. I refuse to give up. I just had to…had to…"

"I know your date with Bobby was just as friends and that you were taking pity on him. If Tucker pulled his head out of his ass, he would have seen that." I really wish I knew what to say to calm her down. I suck at this girl stuff.

"Oh, Emma, I can't wait forever, though! Can't he see that I still love him? If I didn't, I would have moved home by now."

"Oh, hon." I let her cry for a few minutes before I pull her up. "I'm going to go check to see if Cade listened and took Tucker home, then I'm going to tell Bobby and Hank that I'm taking you home. Okay?"

She only nods as I move to leave.

Chapter Three

"THAT'S THE LAST of it," Libby says as she loads the last box into the back end of my truck. We've spent all morning packing up the rest of my room and dismantling my bed to move out to the ranch.

When I got in last night, Tucker was already in bed, but Cade still was watching TV in the living room. We got into an argument that I started about how he needs to be a better friend to Tucker and not let him drink if he plans to stick around. He continued to call me monster, which made my blood boil; I just wanted to hit something.

Thankfully, they are already gone this morning when Libby gets here.

I whistle for Timber, and after she runs over to me, we load up and take off to the ranch. The guys are nowhere to be found so Libby and I begin moving things up to my parents' old bedroom.

Everything was pretty easy to move, except for my bed frame, which is a log bed frame. That sucker is heavy. Libby helps unload all the groceries my mom picked up for us while I start unpacking my room. She has to take off after that, leaving me all alone to reassemble my bed.

"Why in the hell do you have my grandma's log bed frame?" I am just tightening the last bolt when Cade comes walking into my room.

"Because..." I stand up, flip my long blond hair over my shoulder, and glare at him, "your grandma gave it to me."

He huffs out some air and walks around the bed, checking the job I just did. "It was supposed to go to me."

My Cowboy

"Well, maybe if you had stayed here, it would have been yours." I put my tools back in my toolbox and slide it under the now re-made bed. "She thought I would like it so she gave it to me last summer." I throw one of my boxes on my bed, and start to unpack the books onto my bookshelf.

"You've developed a princess complex, I see." Shooting a glare at him over my shoulder, I move back to my bed, trying my best to ignore him as his long, muscled body leans against the wall next to my bathroom door.

"Nope, just a strong-willed bitch." I hear him bark a quick laugh. "Better than an abandoning asshole."

I don't hear anything from him when I carry more books over to my shelf, but when I turned around, he is looming over me with a look in his eyes I can't figure out. I gave him my best murder look, as Libby calls it, that usually sets any guy, including my brother, running.

"I survived." He brings one of his amazing arms up and grabs the shelf behind me. I do a quick once-over of him; tall, amazing set of ripped muscles all encased in a pair of tightly worn Wranglers, and a white shirt that is more like a second skin. I could see that he had a couple of tattoos now; a tribal band around his right arm, and I couldn't quite see the one on his left. He had a cap on today rather than his Stetson. Still quite good looking, except he was pissing me off. "Like you told me to do." He flexes the arm that is right by my head. *Yes, I can see that delicious arm; I'm trying my best not to lick it!*

"How?" I challenge him. "By disappearing and not leaving so much a simple note to explain why?" His cocky grin slips from his face. I may be short, but I have no problem getting in anyone's face.

I square off my shoulders and make myself as tall as I can. "You didn't survive; you ran from everything." I shove past him to start on my next box of books. "You went and became mister big shot bull rider star and left everything to us!" I shove past him again, placing the books on the shelf. "We were here taking care of the arrangements for your dad's funeral which you weren't at." I pass him again. "We took care of your grandma, who, by the way, not only lost her only child, but pretty much her only grandchild as well. I stayed with her. Fourteen years old and I took care of the poor woman."

Cade now stands next to the bookcase in shock of my attitude...I think. "Who cares what you became. I certainly don't, and I know your dad would be pissed at how you acted so selfishly. He didn't raise you like that because I was there!" I poke him hard in the chest, which hurts my finger more than it probably hurt him.

"My dad would be proud of what I've become," he growls back at me. Okay, that is kind of hot, but no way am I going to act on it. I'm over him; I have been for years.

"Bullshit!" I get up in his face the best I can. "He would have wanted you here! Helping my dad, doing what he was doing. You're nothing but a selfish, rotten man now, Cade! I miss the old Cade who cared about everyone and was always there! You lost your dad and gave up and ran away!" I throw my arms up in the air. "You want to talk about surviving! I'm a survivor."

"Yeah and how are you a survivor?" He crosses his arms over his chest causing his muscles to bulge.

I turn back to my bed. "I lost a man who I saw as an uncle; I survived. I lost a boy, one of my best friends, who I cared about a lot; I survived. I lost the person my brother was and fight every day to try and bring him back; I survived!" I violently turn back to face him seeing red. "I lost my dad, too! One of the most important people to me and yet I still SURVIVED! You know nothing about what it takes."

I shove past him to put some things away in my bathroom. I take a deep breath and turn back to him. "I loved you once," I say as calmly as I can. A shocked expression quickly crosses his face

My Cowboy

before he masks it. "With all my heart. I dreamed of the day that you would feel the same. But I got over that real quick, realizing it was just a little girl's stupid dream." I walk with pride back to my bed and sit down.

I calmly take another breath and look up at him. His tan face has gone white, but his eyes have remained the same, an expression I don't understand. "I haven't cried in ten years because of you. I became stronger and vowed never to let tears get in my way. You told me not to cry. Well, guess what, Cade, no matter what shit life has thrown at me. I haven't."

With that, I storm out of my room in search of liquor.

"Emma!" I was almost to the stairs when Cade comes barreling out into the hallway and stomping toward me. He grabs me roughly by my upper arms. I try to ignore the feeling I get when he touches me. I gasp and suck in a quick breath. But I hold my glare in place. "I didn't know what else to do! At the time, I thought my dad would be proud of what I wanted in life!" He slightly pushes me as he lets go. "He wanted a rodeo star, so I gave that to him. I've spent the last ten years doing all that for him." He gestures with his arms.

I roll my eyes, cross my arms, and wait for him to continue. "I came back because I want a life here again. This." He throws his arms up. "This is home. I want to be here again. I'm sorry for the shit I seemed to have caused." He grabs me again and brings me into a hug, leaving me wide-eyed and shocked.

I try my best to keep my body stiff and not melt into his warm embrace. "I didn't think anyone would care," he whispers into my hair. "I wasn't special to anyone but my dad."

As much as part of me wanted to comfort him, the other part won over; tough love. I push myself out of his arms while keeping my temper in check. "You were special to someone besides your dad." He looks almost hopeful. "Your grandma, who probably doesn't even know you're back yet." The hopeful look quickly disappears. "You were special to my parents who saw you as another son. You were special to my brother who couldn't seem to do anything without you, and..." I turn around and start to walk down the stairs. "You were special to me." I don't tell him why, I already did.

~*~*~*~

AN HOUR AFTER the showdown, I come back into the house from the barn. I skipped the alcohol and opted to go take care of Stampede and Ripper. I was grateful that Cade didn't follow me out to continue our bout. I had said what I needed to. I really needed to clear my head, calm the hell down, and try to figure out what that look was in his eyes.

I shouldn't care what he thinks. I shouldn't care about him at all, but I still do. Deep down, under all the hurt and anger I feel toward him, I still want him. Well, the old him, the caring Cade, not this glorified asshole he's become.

My stomach growls as I head toward the kitchen when I smell something delicious cooking; steaks. I enter the kitchen and stop in my tracks. Cade is standing over the stove cooking something I can't see and the sliding glass door is open revealing the barbecue going. I look toward the table and see there are two places set with tea already in the glasses.

I walk around and lean against the counter to see Timber lying at Cade's feet. *Traitor.* "You calmed down now?" he asks as he moves his eyes from the pot of boiling potatoes to me. I nod and continue to watch him. "Good. Now that you got that all out, I would like to have a nice meal with an old friend and catch up."

I nod and move in front of him. "Here, I'll do these. You go take care of the steaks," I all but whisper. I set about mashing the potatoes then move them to the table at the same time he brings the steaks in. "We also need to compare notes on what needs to be done around here." I bend over to pick up my napkin that fell and hear a very manly gasp.

My Cowboy

I stand up straight and turn to see Cade frozen with the plate of steaks in one hand and the tongs in the other. I look down at my outfit, regular tank top in place and a pair of cut-off shorts. *Yeah, that might have been it.* Maybe now, he'll see that I am no longer monster. "Hey, I'm hungry over here!" I wave a hand at him, which seems to do the trick.

I sit in my seat and let out a little laugh. Cade comes over and drops a steak on my plate. "Thank you." I start cutting it up and stop. I stare down at the amazingly cooked steak then up at Cade. "You remembered."

He dazzles me with his smile. "Of course, I remembered. I figured that's one thing that wouldn't change." He starts cutting up his own steak. "I could never figure out how you can eat a steak that is well-done."

"Easy, like this." I take my first bite and can't help but moan. When I open my eyes, he's watching me, frozen again. His eyes are dilated now, and if I'm not mistaken, he is staring at my mouth. "So, what do you want to catch up on?" I tilt my head and stare innocently at him.

It takes him a few seconds to snap out of his daze and bring his eyes back up to mine. "Umm...what have you been up to?"

"Really?" I laugh. "Ten years and that's all you can think of? No, how was the high school experience? Any boyfriends? What did you get this last hunting season?" I throw myself against the back of my chair and wait for him, still laughing.

"Okay...yeah, all that." He grins and takes a bite.

"Well...high school sucked." I take a bite and chew. "I didn't get along with any of the girls and I was always in a fight...along with Libby. I was glad to get the hell out of there. As for boyfriends, none currently. The last dipshit stupid enough to date me just broke it off after cheating on me with Wide Lilly." I take a drink and glance up at him. He's stopped eating and his jaw has got stiff. "That's why I got into a fight with her."

"Want me to kick your ex's ass?"

"HA! No, he isn't worth the trouble." I swallow my next bite. "As for hunting season, I didn't go last year because of Dad. This year, though, I have an elk tag so I'm taking off the end of October to hunt. How's life been treating you?"

He looks confused as he looks up at me. "Don't you know?"

"Know what? Did you get married or something? Because honestly, I didn't care enough to keep track of you. I was too pissed. Dad did, though."

"Really?" He takes his last bite still looking shocked. "I didn't realize it was that bad."

"It was." I put my dishes in the dishwasher and lean against the counter looking at him. "Okay. So, here's the list I have of what I need to get done. Since you're now here to help, I can get the heavy shit out of the way."

- *New Tires on the Tractor*
- *Pasture some of the horses*
- *Repair fence gates in north pastures*
- *Repair stalls in the barn*
- *Misc. repairs around headquarters*

Chapter Four

SUNDAY, JULY 28th, 2013, I became a college graduate, holding a degree in ranch and livestock management. I also became the new owner of the Price Family Ranch. But all this didn't feel official until my mom finally handed me all the books that went with the finances of the ranch.

Most people would feel like this is a huge burden and responsibility at the age of twenty-four but not me, this is what I want for my life. After the argument well, me yelling at Cade we have been getting along. He agreed with my list, adding only a couple things like planting the winter wheat fields.

He made me breakfast this morning. Everything I like bacon, eggs, and waffles with no syrup. The fact that he remembered shocked me and brought my walls down a little, making me a little giddy.

After my graduation, my mom held a barbecue at her house to celebrate. Rebecca, Lee, Libby, Maddi, Tucker, Cade, my mom, and I all gathered in the backyard, enjoying each other's company and telling stories about when we were all younger.

"I remember the night I picked you two up." Lee leans against the picnic table and points at Libby and me. "Joy riding on a tractor down Main Street." He shakes his head.

Libby and I laugh at the same time. "Without driver's licenses." We laugh again.

Cade sits across from me drinking a beer, shaking his head. "You two turned bad."

I wink at him, but Libby is the one to answer. "Someone had to entertain the town. That just fell to Em and me."

"Or there was the time the summer after we graduated high school that we were down skinny dipping in the pond." I smile and take a drink of my tea before I continued. "The wind picked up so much that it blew our clothes away."

Libby, who has had way too much to drink, is sawing back and forth from laughing so hard. "We had to ride back to headquarters naked." She snorts, causing me to start laughing uncontrollably. "Thank God it was dark out by the time we got back." Her laughing gets out of control till she falls backward out of her seat.

"Libby!" I start laughing at her as she continues her laughter on the ground. I turn back to everyone else and see Cade gazing at me. I feel a blush burn across my cheeks so I quickly look down.

"No." Tucker throws himself into the lawn chair next to Maddi and points his bottle of pop between Libby and me. "The best story is your senior prank." He smiles over at Maddi, and she smiles back. Maybe they are finally making progress. "They bought a bunch of chickens out of town so no one could link them, then they released them in the gym on a Friday night after everyone had left with a shit ton of feed. That was three weeks before graduation."

Cade turns from Tucker to me with a brow raised. "The story isn't over," I whispered and looked back at Tucker.

"Then two weeks before graduation, they managed to get some cows and basically did the same thing. No one," Tucker looks up at Lee, "could figure out where all the livestock was coming from." Tucker actually smiles and looks down at his hands before he leans forward. "The week before graduation, they locked the gym so no one could try anything. Monday morning rolls around when the principal walks into his office and finds not one or two but..." He looks at me trying to remember. "Five?" I nod. "Five goats; and they had destroyed his office, eaten everything, and shit everywhere."

"But the best part was graduation." I smile, but it quickly disappears when I look up at my mom.

"How did you top all the livestock?" Cade looks entertained but curious.

"Well, somehow a fox got into the gym during the graduation ceremony. No one knows how it got there, but it ran loose everywhere, making people scream." I grin and bite my lip from laughing again.

Libby, who has now managed to climb back into her seat, finally adds the same part she always does. "And we'll never tell how we did that." She slaps the table and holds her head up with pride.

"No." We all look at my mom who is now smiling. "My favorite is the one where you two managed to talk the whole football team into wear bright pink thongs outside their uniforms for the homecoming game then held an auction for them and donated all the money to breast cancer research." My mom nods and smiles. "That's my favorite."

~*~*~*~

BY THE END of the night, everyone was in a great mood. Tucker was getting comfy with Maddi, which thrilled us, and my mom was even able to talk about my dad without breaking down. *Miracles, I believe in them every day!*

Libby and Cade both were pretty hammered, meaning I had to drive Cade home. He managed to pass out for most of the ride and woke up easily for me when we pulled up to the house.

"Do you need help or can you manage it, cowboy?" I look over at his large frame spread out in my passenger seat and try not to drool.

"No. No." He moves to open the door. "I's got it, monster." Once he finds the handle, he opens the door and falls out.

I roll my eyes, get out of my side, and come around to help him up and walk him up the stairs. "I'm not monster anymore, Cade." I pull him up the best I can and throw his massive arm over my shoulders.

"Oh, don't I know it!" He staggers along but looks down at me with half opened eyes. "You're gorgeous, Emma," he whispers, making my whole body tighten up and a small gasp escape. "Man, you're beautiful. You've got a perfect body." He leans more into me while I try to focus on getting him up the final step and into the house. "See? Perfect for...me," he slurs.

I'm trying to keep my focus and not let him get to me, but I'm failing. I lean him against the wall and go to open the door. "Shut it, Cade. You're drunk and don't know what you're talking about," I mumble after I grab him again.

"Oh, but I do, baby." Chills go up my back. I'm just going to dump him on the couch and run up to my room. "It just sucks that I can't do anything about your tiny little amazing body and what it does to me."

"Oh, yeah, and why is that?" I lower him onto the couch and go to step back. But I trip on the rug and fall right on top of him. I push myself up off his chest and look wide-eyed into his.

"Because you're my best friend's baby sister," he whispers as he looks down at my lips. His hands snake around my waist pulling me up closer to his face.

My nipples begin to harden as they rub against his hard chest while we breathe. He starts to slowly move toward my lips, and ever so lightly brushes his against mine. I feel a jolt of electricity shoot from him to me and down to my core. *Oh. My. God.* His kisses are the sweetest ones I have ever gotten. He doesn't push to move past what we are doing.

My Cowboy

When I let out a small moan, Cade pulls back and looks into my eyes with a smile. "Now I can have those sweet kisses to remember and to dream about." His eyes close and his head falls back on the couch with a thud.

Seriously! I lay against his chest for about a minute waiting for him to open his eyes and to continue kissing me, but nothing happens except that he starts snoring. "Seriously?" I shout, but it doesn't do any good. "Men." I shove myself off his chest and storm up to my room, slamming the door shut.

It's only after I've changed and crawled into bed that I calm down. I touch my lips to feel his kiss still there. With a smile, I close my eyes and go to sleep.

~*~*~*~

THE NEXT MORNING, I make my way down for breakfast with caution. *Will he remember last night or won't he* is the main question going through my mind. If he does, will he say it was a mistake?

I shake my head as I walk into the kitchen and find that Cade is not up making breakfast. Shrugging, I set about making it myself while I let Timber out the sliding door.

I'm in the process of whipping up some scrambled eggs when he arrives. Even though I feel him before I see him, I don't stop what I'm doing. "Morning." I freeze for a second. God, his voice is sexy in the morning, all rough and dry from sleeping.

"Morning," I say as I pour the eggs in. "Something greasy for breakfast for your stomach?" I look over my shoulder at him and smile.

He gives me a quick smile and scratches his head. "That would be great." I watch him stretch before I turn back to the eggs.

"Okay. Go get cleaned up, I'm about done." He doesn't reply when he leaves. Well, so far he hasn't said anything.

After the eggs cooked, I serve everything up on two plates and put them at the table with coffee and orange juice. I'm about to sit down when he comes back in pulling his shirt over his head. *How do you eat again?* I stare down at my food and frown.

"Something wrong?"

I look up at him and shake my head. "Just forgot the pepper." Quickly, I grab it and add it to my meal.

"What in the hell happened last night?" he asks as he takes his seat and prepares his food to eat.

"What do you mean?"

"I don't remember getting back here. Did I drive?"

"Ha! Hell, no. I brought you back. Then I deposited you on the couch because I honestly don't think I'm strong enough to get you up the stairs."

"Yeah." He lets out a little laugh. "You're probably right about that, monster."

I drop my fork. *I'm monster again? I want to be baby.* "You okay?"

Again, I look up at him. "No. I'm not." I go back to my food. "I'm not a monster anymore, Cade. No one calls me that, so I would greatly appreciate it if you would stop." I cut into my eggs and violently shove some into my mouth.

"Okay." He looks at me. "I won't call you that anymore, Emma."

"Thank you." We eat in silence; part of me is sad that he doesn't remember, but the other part is relieved. I don't think I could handle what he would have to say about the kissing. Once I'm done, I go to stand. "If you're up for it, I'll meet you down at the barn, and we will get started working."

I basically flee from the house.

~*~*~*~

HALF AN HOUR later, we are fixing the last gate to the north pasture. "Fence-line looks good." Cade stands up straight, removing his hat and wiping his forehead. For a morning at the end of July, it's warming up already.

My Cowboy

"Yeah." I stand up and remove my gloves. "I try my best to keep the inner fences in shape. The neighbors help me with the borders." I point out to some of the border fence that we can just barely see.

Cade goes about testing the gate to make sure it will hold. Working on them hasn't been that difficult, but the heat is making us sweat. Sweaty Cade is a glorious sight. Even though he is wearing a darker shirt, the sweat causes it to cling to every curve of his muscular chest and abs.

I know they are there, I felt them last night. Speaking of last night, he still hasn't let on to anything. And I have mixed feelings about it.

As I sit on my four-wheeler, I watch a bead of sweat roll down his arm. How I would love to lick that off...I look up to Cade's eyes and see that he is watching me closely with a shit-eating grin on his face.

"You okay there, sugar?" *Sugar?* My body tingles at that. *Emma likes!*

I hide that response and frown. "Yeah. Why?"

"You're dazin'." He leans against the four-wheeler he drove out. "I asked if the fair and rodeo still come around here this month?"

"Well, duh." I move to start my four-wheeler. "Don't forget the dance on Main Street afterward. That's all tradition." I look past him and see some cows moving toward us. "We'll need to move them, maybe tomorrow?" I nod to them and wait for his answer.

"Sure. Sounds good." He climbs up and gets ready to start his. "You still go to all that?"

"What, the fair and rodeo? Of course, they contract some of my bulls." I look back at the cattle and see the telltale signs of Roundhouse. "There is one of them now." I hop off and whistle for him, making him pick up speed to get to me.

"You're contracting?"

I look back at him. "Yeah, side income. Dad and I were really considering doing more before he passed." I turn back and Roundhouse is right there. "Hey, boy." I walk up and run my hand up his face, earning me a nudge from his nose at my hand. "Missed you, too." I kiss it and turn back to Cade. "This is Roundhouse. My best bull and another one of my babies."

He is now walking toward us with another grin on his face. "How many babies do you have?"

"Well, there is Stampede and Ripper, but they were Gema's babies before they were mine."

"I remember her. Where is she?"

I pick some dried mud off Roundhouse. "She died giving birth to them. If you'd taken a close enough look at them, you would have figured out who their dad is." I look over Roundhouse's head to see Cade walking around him.

"Who?" he asks as he bends over to look at Roundhouse.

"Scooter."

He shoots up straight. "My Scooter?"

I laugh and nod. "Yep, broke into Gema's pen and knocked her up. And now he and Ripper fight over some of the other mares."

He laughs and shakes his head. "Well, wouldn't that make Stampede and Ripper mine? Care to share custody?"

"Ha! No, Scooter was just the sperm donor. Those boys are mine." I look back into Roundhouse's eyes.

"Any other babies?" When I look up again, Cade is standing on the other side of Roundhouse's head looming over me. I simply nod. "Who?" he whispers. His eyes have grown dark…why?

I grin and point over my shoulder to Timber, who is currently rolling in a cow pie.

He laughs. "Glad I don't have to clean her up." He moves back to his four-wheeler. "He's a mighty fine bull, Emma."

My Cowboy

Not a fine as you. I pet Roundhouse one last time and move to my four-wheeler. "Load up, Timber." She's still trying to master how to get on without falling off the other side. "It's dry, she'll clean herself." I look over at him. "Check fence line in a couple of days?"

He laughs. "May take a few days."

I shrug. "So what, we have nothing but time." I wink at him.

We start up the four-wheelers and head for home.

Chapter Five

One Week Later

"SO, WHAT HAPPENED with Tucker?" I look up from my stall over to the one that Cade is working on. It's been a week, and we've started to reconnect our friendship. However, I still hold the secret to the amazing kissing action we had that night.

"What do you mean?"

"Well, everything?" He goes back to moving hay.

I take a deep breath and lean against my pitchfork. "On his fourth tour in the East, his truck was hit by a roadside bomb. He was up in the gun turret, so his injuries weren't as bad as some of the other guys, and he survived. But he lost his leg and was scarred pretty badly."

Cade now leans up against the wall between us looking all sexy with his shirt off and tucked into the back pocket of his tight Wranglers, and his baseball cap on backward. "Yeah, I get that part. I mean, why is he so different?"

"PTSD," I simply state as I go back to work. "He was fine after they shipped him back state side. He went through several surgeries and physical therapy back East. Maddi stayed by his side the whole time. They met after he was in boot camp in Virginia. Anyways, after he was well enough to come home, she came with him." I walk out of the stall and head toward the next one. "He was depressed since he couldn't ride, but he still helped out where he could. Then Dad was diagnosed with lung cancer."

My Cowboy

Cade follows me out and stands at the door of the stall, shaking his head. "I am sorry about your dad." He crosses his arms and gives me a weak smile.

"It is what it is. But Dad's death made Tucker worse." I set my pitchfork against the wall and lean against the wall next to it, looking at Cade. "His moods used to come and go, nothing too bad, but after Dad died..." I shake my head and look down. When I look back up, Cade is standing right in front of me, clenching and releasing his fists. "He got really down after Dad was diagnosed. He broke off his engagement with Maddi, refused to help me out here, and hasn't been the same since."

I look back down and shake my head. Cade's arms come around me and encase me in his strong embrace. "He'll come back, sugar," he whispers to the top of my head.

I can't breathe. My whole body jolts just from his touch. I want nothing more than to melt into his body, but *I know he is probably just trying to be brotherly...dammit!*

"I know." I breathe. I manage to look up at him, giving him my best doe eyes. *Kiss me, please!* I never beg for anything; I either take what I want or work my ass off for it, but I'd beg Cade.

He stares down at me for a spell then moves his hands to my shoulders. *Oh, for the love of God, kiss me!* He smiles, then pats my shoulders and goes back to work.

For shit's sake, not again! All last week, he acted as if he wanted to kiss me when he was close but never did. *Dammit!*

"Maybe you being around again will bring my brother back," I say low but not so much that he can't hear me.

"I'll try my best to help, Emma." He offers me a reassuring smile then disappears into his stall.

~*~*~*~

AN HOUR LATER, I'm making my way into the final stall while Cade repairs some of the doors of the other stalls. I'll be the first to admit that the cowboy at the other end of the barn sexually frustrates me.

I had removed my over shirt and was now just in my tank top and cut-off shorts with my Muck boots. Yep, I look sexy. Well, Cade must think so because I keep catching him staring at my ass.

I wasn't paying close enough attention to where I was stepping, and suddenly found myself on my back. I lie there in horse shit staring up at the ceiling trying to figure out what just happened. I'm stunned, to say the least.

As I get ready to get up and shake off my fall, Cade is suddenly over me looking extremely worried. "Jesus, Emma. Are you okay?" He takes my hand and pulls me up till I'm standing.

I look up at him, still stunned, and try to nod my head. "Ouch." I finally shake out of it and I start to pat my back. "Shit." I throw my head back and close my eyes.

"What!" I look back at Cade to see his standing really close wide-eyed and concerned.

"Shit." I turn around. "I'm covered in it." I start to walk off; *I need to clean myself off.*

"Wait, Emma!" Cade grabs my arm and pulls me back to him. I slide again and fall into his chest. "Shit!" He topples over, right into the pile I just got out of.

Once again, I'm on my back staring up at the ceiling, but this time I'm on top of Cade. I shake my head and let out a laugh as I go to get up. "Well, cowboy." I turn to look down at him. *Shirtless covered in horse shit and still sexy.* "Looks like we need to hose off."

I offer my hand to help him up. "Just great," he says as he gets up.

"What? It's not like you had a hot date or anything." I turn around and start to head for the hose. "Come on."

As we reach the hose, I pull my tank top off to reveal that I have a camouflage bikini top on. Now, I just have to wash my hair and my ass. After I finish hosing off, I go to hand the hose to Cade, but he doesn't take it.

I look up through the water drops that are falling on my face to see him standing over me staring down at me with a heated look. His fists are clenched at his sides, and his chest is tight. *Yum.*

As much as I want to jump him, I control myself. And by control myself, I mean I turn the hose on him.

When I pull the hose away from his face, he's shocked first then turns to a grin. "Oh! You're gettin' it now!" He makes a grab for it, but I drop it and take off.

I'm laughing hard when he catches me. He wraps one of his arms around my waist, hoisting me into the air. "Cade!" I scream as I fly back down. He catches me then throws me over his shoulder. "Oh, my God! Cade put me down!" I playfully beat on his back then brace myself on him.

He stops moving for a brief second the moment my hands touch his bare back, which, by the way, is still covered in shit.

I manage to get up a little to see where he is taking me. When I see the horse trough, my eyes go big; I know what's coming. "No way in hell, Cade! That water is cold!"

He gives me a hard smack on my ass. "Just the point. You need to cool off."

"Hell, no!" I start to move to get out of his arms, but all I do is make him laugh. He's too strong. "Seriously, Cade, no! I'm sorry."

He lifts me up by my waist and starts to hurl me into it, but I have other plans. I manage to wrap my legs around him and pull him in with me. "Emma!" he yells as he topples in on top of me.

I go under. *Okay, I didn't think this through.* He moves a little to pull me back up above the water. I cough and wipe my eyes. I look up at him with a smile and start to laugh. When he starts to laugh with me, I freeze and stare at him.

He's straddling me, and with his laughing, he is moving back and forth up against me. My lower parts start to tighten, and I try to squeeze my legs together.

I bite my lip when he looks back down at me with a huge smile. He stops laughing and licks his lips.

Please, for the love of God, kiss me before I explode! His chest is rising and falling evenly, but not mine. Mine is going crazy, which catches his eye. He looks down my parts that he can see through the water then back up to my face.

This time I lick my lips. He ever so slowly starts to bring his face down to mine when...a truck horn sounds. "Hey!" Shit, it's Tucker!

Cade's eyes go big, and he quickly gets off me and out of the trough. He gives me his hand to help me out.

Once I'm out, I look up at my brother who is now glaring at Cade. "What the fuck is going on?" He shoots daggers at both of us.

Cade looks down at me and I shrug. "Just cooling off, Tuck." I move past him. "Chill out."

It's best for me to walk away. Otherwise, I will make my brother pissed at his best friend.

~*~*~*~

It'S TWO A.M. by the time I get home the next morning. *Thank God, that was my last shift ever at Hank's.* I love working there, but between trying to get the ranch back together all day and going to work all night at the bar, it is too much. I'm twenty-four years old...I need to live a little.

I stretch and yawn as I walk up the porch to the front door. Once inside, I see that the light in the living room is on.

I smile at the sight in front of me and let out a little laugh. Cade is asleep on the couch in front of the television with a beer bottle in his hand.

My Cowboy

I walk over, shut off the television, and manage to get the bottle out of his hand. I don't think he's going to wake up. I move to grab the blanket I leave on the back of the couch to cover him up.

I look up at him and stop with the blanket in my hands. He's watching me. "Hey," I whisper and go to stand back.

"Hey," he whispers back as grabs my arm and pulls me down onto his lap.

"What are you doing?"

He smiles. "Why are you still whispering?"

I look up into his eyes. "I'm not sure."

He tilts his head to the side, regarding me, and pushes a piece of my hair behind my ear. He then lets his hand slowly trail down my cheek and the side of my neck where it stops.

"You really have become an amazing and beautiful woman, Emma." He wraps his hand around my neck and brings my face closer to his. I gasp at the movement. "I'm going to kiss you, sugar," he whispers as he brings his lips to mine.

The same jolt travels back through me as he lightly brushes his lips against mine. He then rubs his tongue against my bottom lip asking for entrance to my mouth. When I do, his kisses turn fierce and make me moan.

I snake my arms around his neck and bring myself up closer to him. I start to wrestle my tongue with his, and when I pull back for a quick second, I take his bottom lip with me between my teeth.

With hooded eyes, I look up at him, back to his lips and back up again. "Please tell me that you aren't drunk," I whisper while I move to kiss his jaw line up to his ear.

He lets out a small brief laugh against my neck. "No, sweetheart, I'm not."

I lightly bite down on his ear and pull on it. "Then what took you so long?" He runs his hands down my sides and then back up causing me to shiver and my nipples to go hard.

He kisses my neck then pulls his head back to look me in the eye. "I wanted your brother's permission."

I frown. "Tucker isn't my keeper." I cross my arms over my chest causing my breasts to push up a little under my tight Hank's shirt.

"I know that." He grabs a strand of hair and plays with it. "But I also know that he is really protective of you. I wanted him to know my interest and that I would never hurt you." He kisses my nose. "Never again."

As sweet as all this is, it also pisses me off because he felt the need to ask my brother. Reminds me too much of Trey, the stupid douche bag ex. I move to get off his lap, away from his warmth that I already miss, and away from his hard-on that I so badly wanted to ride rubbing against my legs. "'Night."

"Wait!" He scrambles to get up. "Emma, wait!"

I'm halfway up the stairs when he catches me. I whirl around and glare up at him. "Listen here, Cade." I poke him in the chest. "I do what I want, and I never ask my brother for permission on anything." I shake my head. "As much as I would like to continue what we started, I'm backing off and going to bed."

"Why?" Now he's pissed. *Well, welcome to my world.*

I turn and start to climb the stairs again. "Because you had to ask my brother for permission. Sorry, Cade, but I'm sick of dealing with guys who care what my brother thinks and are often times scared of him. I want someone who will just take what they want and make me feel special." I look over my shoulder at him. "'Night." I walk into my room, shut the door and just stand there. *What in the hell did I just do?*

Chapter Six

THE NEXT MORNING I got up super early and escaped to the barn. I had to get one of my boys saddled up to get my bulls rounded up for the rodeo starting Friday. I was relieved that Cade wasn't up yet. I tossed and turned all night thinking about how I walked away from him.

Well, I'm not backing down. If he wants me bad enough, he will figure out how to get me.

When I walk into the barn, my boys look up from their stalls at me. "Morning, lovelies." I kiss both of them on the nose and move to open Ripper's stall.

My phone starts to ring, making Ripper rear back and start to freak out. "Hey boy, settle down." I frown up at him. "Maybe I shouldn't take you; you're skittish right now." I back out of his stall and move over to Stampede's as I answer my phone. "Morning, doll. Aren't you up a little early?"

"Fuck you. I can't get this amazing body by sleeping in." Libby puffs as she runs along her street with her Bluetooth in.

"Love it when you talk dirty to me, Lib." I laugh as I lead Stampede out.

"Shut it. Soooo ..."

"So?"

"How's the cowboy?"

I hold the phone between my ear and my shoulder as I move to throw the blanket over Stampede's back then my saddle. "Fine, why?"

"Well, just wondering. Has he remembered that kiss yet?" Poor, poor Libby. She has no sausage, her word not mine, at the moment, so she has to find a way to fill it.

"No, but he should remember the one he gave me last night."

"WHAT!" I pull the phone away and wince.

"He pulled me onto his lap and kissed me last night."

"OH. My. God!" I can tell she has stopped running and probably looks like a crazy woman on the side of the road.

"Yeah, well then he told me that he asked Tucker for permission and I couldn't take it." I sigh and move the phone to my other ear. "I don't need another Trey."

"Ummm...No." She pauses. "I thought Cade would be all bull rider on that."

"What does that mean?" I start to cinch my saddle down.

"You know, ride ya hard, fast, and maybe spur you if he gets kinky."

"Ooh God, Libby." I roll my eyes.

"No! Oh God, Cade!" she shouts.

"Well, it ain't happening unless he mans up." I check to see if the saddle is good. "I'm tired of guys who either try to appease my brother or are scared of him. I want one who will take charge and not care what my brother thinks, only what I think and cares for me."

"You want a caveman with a heart?"

"Yep." I swing up on top of Stampede and take off. "Now, I'm off to get my bulls."

"Wait!"

"What Lib?"

"So does that mean no vagina hugs for Cade?"

I pull back on Stampede's reins to a stop, pull my phone from my ear, and glare down at it. "A what?" I ask after I pull it back to my ear.

"You know, a vagina hug. Where your..."

"Okay, okay, I got it. Where in the hell did you hear that?"

"Oh, it just came to me one day. I do like the shock factor that comes with saying it." I roll my eyes. *This girl doesn't surprise me anymore.*

"No. No vagina hugs for Cade...for now." She squeals. "I'm going to lose you here real soon Libby. I'll talk to you later."

"Okay. Loves ya!"

"Love ya, too." I hang up and bend back to put my phone in my saddlebag.

~*~*~*~

Later That Night

I LAY ON the horn for the fourth time waiting on Maddi and Libby to come out of the house. "Come on, you two! I'm going to be late!"

"Slow your roll, girly," Libby says as her and Maddi slide in. "You'll make it in time."

I roll my eyes and start the truck. "Says the girl who is getting in for free and gets all the drinks she wants...also for free!"

"Damn straight!" She winks and claps her hands.

"Is Tucker coming this year?" Maddi leans forward to look at me.

I glance over at her and give her the best smile I can. "I don't think so. Mom and I are trying to keep him away from anything close to drinking."

She gives a quick smile but then looks away sad. I wish I could just snap my brother out of it and get them back together, but it's something they need to do together.

We pull in through the contestants' entrance and park my truck in the back by the bullpens. When I get out, I look over and smile at my boys. They look great this year. As the owner of them, I want them all to buck their riders off, but as a fan of the sport, I hope that at least some get scores. I pat Wild Card's head and walk off to get all my shit together and the line up for what order my bulls go in.

I climb up top Stampede to get ready for my announcement in the opening ceremony of the rodeo. *Time to plaster on a fake-ass smile!*

"Welcome, ladies and gentlemen, to the annual Elk Field Rodeo!" The grandstands go crazy with rodeo fans cheering. Okay, maybe my smile isn't fake. "Who's ready to rock and roll on this amazing Friday night?" The announcer is getting the crowd going.

I move Stampede up to the gates where we will be running through. First, the local cowboy band goes out and starts playing some music while the announcer announces the rodeo royalty. "Now, all you locals will know this young lady." The crowd has calmed down a bit. "She grew up right here in Elk Field and now is producing some mighty fine bulls for our riders to ride and all at the age of twenty-four!" I take a deep breath. "Give a hometown welcome to Emma Price of Price Rodeo Company!" The crowd cheers as I kick Stampede and we take off in a full run into the arena.

As we run around the arena, I smile and wave at all the people who are here. In the years past, I used to be a flag girl, so riding out in this arena is nothing. But it feels amazing now that everyone knows me. This is something my dad dreamed of.

Once I'm in my spot, I wave a few more times and then wait. "Good boy." I lean down and rub the side of Stampede's neck. I had planned to bring Ripper, but he's been jumpy lately.

Once all the sponsors are announced and the national anthem plays, it's time to start the rodeo. I have a long wait, so I go back behind the chutes and see who drew which bull.

I'm halfway down the list when I freeze.

Cade Masters......Roundhouse

Cade? Cade is riding tonight? He didn't tell me. Well, actually we really haven't talked since last night. We catch each

My Cowboy

other looking at one another, but the words don't come, just heated looks. He busied himself with our list while I was busy getting everything ready for this weekend.

"Hey, sugar." A chill goes up my back. I turn around and look up into the glorious brown eyes of Cade.

"Hey." I bite my lip and look away.

He lifts my chin with his strong finger till I'm looking up at him again. Before I can say anything, he leans down and gives me a quick kiss on the lips. When he's satisfied, he smiles down at me. "For luck," he whispers then walks off.

~*~*~*~

I'M WATCHING ALL the bull riders getting ready up on the chute above my bulls. I'm nervous; I'll admit it. I pace back and forth, biting my nails. Libby and Maddi are back in the beer garden getting drunk, and I wish I could be with them.

"Now, ladies and gents, on to everyone's favorite event." The crowd gets loud. "Elk Field, are you ready for bull riding on this Friday night!?!" The crowd goes crazy. I smile a bit but look down at my boys. They'll do great.

I stop at the chute Roundhouse is in. He's one of my babies, and I'm a little nervous that Cade got him. Okay, actually, I'm pissed. Cade has spent the last ten years riding bulls in the PBR, and I want Roundhouse to do amazing.

"Calm down, baby." Cade's voice comes to my ear, causing my anxiety to be forgotten as my panties dampen.

I nervously smile up at him. "I'm calm," I lie.

He turns me to face him. "No, you're not. Come here." He pulls me down the ramp and out of the view of the public. Before I can ask where we are going, Cade pulls me into his arms and kisses me. Not no sweet, chaste kiss. This kiss is all consuming, deadly, and hot as hell. I give back what he is giving me. Our teeth are crashing into one another as our tongues battle for dominance. I let out a long sweet moan, making him smile against my mouth.

When he pulls back, the smile is still there. "How's that, baby?"

I'm dazzled and can't seem to speak. I just want to bring him back down to me and continue kissing him.

"Now, ladies and gents, you may know this man. He grew up right here in Elk Field and for the last ten years has made a name for himself in the PBR."

"Gotta go, baby." He kisses me once more then climbs up the chutes to get on Roundhouse.

Slowly, I come back to myself and make my way up there to watch him.

"Give a big welcome home to Cade Masters!" The crowd cheers as Cade waves to all of them then climbs down on the back of Roundhouse.

He's such a big guy, muscles everywhere. Making it hard for anyone not to eye fuck him. I hear some women yelling at him how much they love him and want to marry him. I start to get a little jealous till I look at him, and he gives me a wink before he nods that he is ready.

Roundhouse does a high, all-four-legs-off-the-ground kick right out of the chute then goes into a right spin bucking back and forth trying to get Cade off him. They move amazingly well together.

Cade spurs his sides and manages to stay on top of him for at least three seconds till he starts to slide. But he manages to get righted and continues to ride. Before I know, it the buzzer goes off and Cade moves to get off Roundhouse.

He manages to get up on his feet before Roundhouse turns to chase after him. Cade manages to jump up on the side of the chutes and out of the way quickly, leaving Roundhouse to turn back and go out the exit.

I smile and shake my head. *Leave it to my boy to get mad at my cowboy. Wait...no, not mine. Cade is not mine...yet.*

My Cowboy

Cade smiles and winks up at me as they announce his score of eighty-six. Not bad for our small time rodeo. I'm proud of both of them. He jumps over and runs his hand down my cheek. "I'll wait for you out back, baby." With that, he walks off while I continue to watch the rest of my bulls either be ridden or buck off their riders.

After my last bull bucked off his rider, I make my way to go find Cade and see what his plans are for the rest of the night.

I stop when I see a bunch of girls gathered around Cade smiling and vying for his attention. He smiles down them, signs some autographs, and laughs at something one said.

I clench my fists to my sides, and my blood starts to boil. *Fuck this shit.* I turn around and storm off. I'll go home and drink my pain away. He can do whatever the fuck he wants.

Once I'm home, I strip out of my rodeo clothes and put on a sports bra and shorts. I stomp around the house, which seems to excite Timber. I grab a full bottle Southern Comfort. "Come on, baby girl; let's go watch a scary movie." I pick up Timber and head up to my room. Watching something scary while drinking always cheers me up.

Chapter Seven

LAST NIGHT, I fell asleep with my movie on full blast and my bedroom door locked, so if Cade tried to knock or come in, I wouldn't hear him. Besides, after I drank a third of my bottle, I passed out.

This morning, I hurried to get my stuff together. I had the bulls to take care of today, and then I planned to get ready at my mom's house. I also packed the shirt I was going to change into for the dance.

Cade tried to call me throughout the day, so by the time I got to the fairgrounds, I had powered my phone down and thrown it in my passenger seat.

After the opening ceremony, I go behind the chutes again to see who has drawn which of my bulls.

Cade Masters......Thunder Catcher

Ha! He just happened to draw one of my more temperamental bulls. I have a hard time even being around Thunder Catcher. With a little spring in my step, I head to the beer garden to get a beer and celebrate.

Tonight, I don't stick around the chutes for fear of running into Cade. I really don't feel like having it out with him. Instead, I plan to find someone to make him jealous with; if it will even work.

I walk around the grandstands, stop and talk with people I know, and even with some that I don't.

After barrel racing, I head back over to the chutes to watch my bulls and try to stay clear of Cade. I'm halfway over to the other

My Cowboy

side when he comes out on Thunder Catcher. "Buck 'em!" I yell at my bull and sure as shit, he throws Cade.

I step back feeling a little guilty for the joy that I feel. I shrug it off and continue walking. Once on the other side, I lean against one of the gates to watch.

"Well, well, well. Look at that mighty fine back-side." I shake my head and smile at the sound of a very familiar voice.

I turn around and smile up at Justin Foster, bronc rider and former boyfriend. "Long time, no see, good lookin'." I walk over and give him a hug.

"Yeah, well, being a pro bronc rider keeps me away." He laughs as he holds me at arm's length. "You're lookin' great, missy."

"Not too bad yourself." I wink at him and punch him in the arm.

He looks past me making his smile vanish. "I see that Masters is back in town." I look over my shoulder to see Cade glaring at Justin. *Perfect. Just what I need*. Justin and I ended our relationship because we realized we were better off as friends, but Cade doesn't know that.

I turn back and smile up at Justin. "So, you going down to the dance?" I walk my fingers up his chest.

"You know it!" He smiles again at me.

"Okay, well I've already started drinking and shouldn't drive..." I trail off.

"Want to ride with me?"

"If you don't mind Libby and Maddi riding with us."

"You know I don't." His smile gets bigger. *I know he has a thing for my best friend.*

I nod. "Okay. Let's go find them." He throws an arm over my shoulders and we take off toward the beer garden leaving Cade glaring and brooding.

~*~*~*~

I AM ON, I believe, my fifth Southern Comfort and Dr. Pepper. I really am not keeping track. This is the one time every year that I let myself go. Well, ever since I turned twenty-one.

I've been spending the evening dancing mainly with Libby and Maddi but also with Justin. By midnight, I am feeling pretty good and having a blast.

Justin had excused himself about ten minutes ago and came back with drinks for us girls. "Ladies," he says as he hands us all our drinks and then starts dancing with me again.

I think he drank more than I have because he is dancing way too close to me. He bends down and starts to whisper in my ear, well, shouts over the music, "Want to get out of here?!?"

I'm about to answer when I feel electric jolt run through me. "She ain't going anywhere with you, Foster." I look up from my drink to see Cade and Tucker looming over us. *Party police!*

Tucker glares down at me then turns to Maddi and Libby. "Maddi, Lib, time to go." He turns and starts walking. Libby doesn't plan to leave, but Maddi falls right into step with him. *Traitor.*

I chance a look up at Cade, who is now holding out his hand to me. "Fuck off, Cade!" I turn around only for him to hoist me into the air and over his shoulder. "Dammit! Put. Me. Down." I beat on his back with every word, which only earns me a hard slap on the ass. "Cade Nathan Masters, put me down this instance!"

"Not happenin', sugar." He carries me through the crowd and out the gate. I continue to yell at him till we reach his truck, which is parked clear out in bum fuckin' nowhere!

Once we are at his truck, he lowers me to the ground then pins me against the side.

"Let me go, Cade!" I yell up at his face.

He isn't smiling; he's pissed. *Why?* "What the hell were you trying to pull with Foster back there?"

"What the hell do you mean? I was having fun!" I stomp my foot. Yes, like a kid, I stomp it.

My Cowboy

He rubs one hand down his face. "He's a man-whore, Emma!"

"Takes one to know one!"

"What the fuck does that mean!" He gets closer to my face.

I punch him a couple times in the chest, but it does no good. "You! Last night with those girls!" I drop my hands and fall back against the truck. Damn him for being so strong and sexy.

He lifts my chin and forces me to look at him. "They were just fans, baby."

"I'm not your baby!"

"Emma! Knock it off." He lifts my chin again. "Dammit. Is that why you're doing this? To make me jealous because you were last night?" I try to look away and not answer. "It is, isn't it? Oh baby, I was just appeasing the fans." He turns my head so I look into his eyes. "I only see you, Emma. Okay?"

I glare up at him but nod my head. "Can I go back to having fun now?"

He laughs and shakes his head. "You've had too much to drink." He leans in and kisses me sweetly on the lips. One taste and I'm done for.

I reach my arms up and around his neck as he starts to pull away. I open my mouth and invite his tongue in. While our tongues move in a dance, he lifts me up against his truck and pushes himself into my center. It's all I can do to wrap my legs around his waist and grind myself against him.

"Oh, God. Cade." I pull back and look into his eyes. "I want you." I grind against him again causing him to let out a long low hiss.

"Fuck, Emma." He fists my shirt, pulling it up a little to reveal my stomach then runs his fingers down my side.

"Cade. Please," I beg between kisses.

He moves slightly away from me. His eyes are hooded and dark. "Emma. I really want to take my time."

"I don't." I grind against him again. "Please, Cade." My voice has gone all out sexy on me.

"Fuck!" He throws his head back. After about a minute, he looks back down at me and kisses me hard and fast. He moves one of my legs and starts digging in his pocket. I don't realize it's his keys till I hear the door unlock. "I'm going to fuck you in my truck, baby, and then I'm taking you home and taking my time on you." He kisses me one last time then moves open the door.

Once the door is open, he quickly tosses me onto the back seat and makes quick work of my pants. "Oh, baby, were you expecting something tonight?" He's staring down below.

I frown. "No why?"

"Those are the sexiest damn underwear I've ever seen and black, too. Emma, I approve." He licks his bottom lip and he crawls in with me, shutting the doors behind him.

"I always wear this kind of thong."

He stops undoing his belt and looks down, shocked at me. Then gives me a panty-melting grin. "God, working with you during the day just got harder."

I bite my lip and shake my head.

I reach up and start working on his pants because he is going way to slow for me. "Emma!" He's shocked as I try to rip his pants off.

"I need you now, Cade!" After his pants and boxer briefs are down, I grab him and pull him toward me. I brush a kiss across his mouth before biting down on his lower lip.

"Fuck, Emma." He picks me up and moves so I'm now straddling him. "You wet for me, baby?" He trails his fingers down my sides, and they soon disappear into my thong.

"Wet?" I shake my head. "No, sweetheart, I'm soaked." I start to moan as he rubs his fingers against my clit. "Ooooo."

My Cowboy

He moves his fingers closer to my core and slowly inserts one finger, then two, and finally, three. "Man, Emma." He starts pumping his fingers leisurely in and out of me while his thumb rubs my clit. Then he hooks his fingers to my left side, and I lose it.

"God! Yes, Cade!" I start to ride his fingers faster as he rubs against my spot. This excites me; no one has ever found it before. I start to ride them faster, bucking uncontrollably until I feel myself go over the edge. "Cade!" I scream as my orgasm rips through me.

I rock a couple more times, and then bring my head back to look down at him.

He licks his bottom lip. "You look amazing when you come, Emma." I smile at him and run my hand down his cheek, lovingly.

"It's been a while."

"Well, I ain't done with you yet." He kisses the side of my neck. The next thing I know, I'm on my back with Cade slowly sliding into me. He hisses through his teeth as his rather large member slides into my tight center. "You're right; you're tight, baby."

I raise one of my legs over his shoulder to give him more. Once he is all the way in, he rocks back and forth a few times to get me use to his size. "Ready for me to fuck you, Emma?" All I can do is nod.

Just like when he rides a bull, the second the I nod, the bucking begins. Cade's thrusts are hard and relentless as he slams into me, causing all thoughts to leave my head, air from my lungs, and I just try to hold on.

There is no gentle loving; with every thrust, his balls slap against me and soon the sounds of wet skin slapping against wet skin fill the cab of the truck.

"Ooooo." I move my head back exposing my neck to him. He moves down and starts to lightly bite and kiss it while still punishing me. "F-f-fuck Cade!" I try to manage saying something, but I fail.

Again, I feel myself reaching the edge. As I start to fall, I meet his thrusts with my own and clamp down on him. "Emma." His voice strains from trying to hold on.

Once my orgasm hits me, I throw my head back and scream out his name, soon hearing my own coming from him.

He pumps a few more times into me slowly, then stops. I open my eyes and smile up at him. We are both trying to catch our breath but failing.

After a couple minutes, I reach up and wipe the sweat from his forehead. "Wow," is all I can manage.

He nods. "Wow is right." He kisses my hand as it comes down from his face. Then he pulls out of me. I miss the feel of him already.

He starts to work his pants back into place while I attempt to sit up. "Good thing I parked clear out here." He winks at me as he moves to open the door to get out.

I reach for my underwear only to find that in the rush of it all, he ripped them off. "You ripped one of my favorite pairs, you savage." I smile up at him then put my pants back on.

I climb out after him and breathe in some fresh air. "I'll get you more." He slaps my butt and moves to get into the driver's seat. "Let's go home." He winks as he climbs in.

I get into the truck and start to buckle up when he stops me. "What are you doing over there? Get your ass over here." He pulls me to him. He takes my hand and kisses it. "You're mine now, Emma. All mine."

"Then you're mine," I say back earning a smile.

"You bet your sweet ass on that." He starts up the truck after I buckle up and takes off.

I smile to myself. *Well, I got what I wanted. Now, the question is whether I can handle it.*

Chapter Eight

I YAWN AND START to stretch. *Oh, it feels so good.* I go to turn to get out of bed when it occurs to me that my waist has something wrapped around it.

Opening my eyes with a frown, I look over my shoulder to see a very naked Cade facing me and breathing evenly.

I jump out of bed in shock and somehow manage not to wake him. *What in the hell?* I shake my head as last night comes back to me. *Oh, yeah.* A shit-eating grin comes to my face as I remember him hauling me to the truck then what happened after we got back here.

He carried me up to my room then proceeded to love me slowly for the rest of the night before we collapsed in exhaustion. A tired but satisfied grin comes across my face thinking back to how tender and loving this cowboy was with me last night.

I spent the majority of my lifetime pining over this man, wanting him to love me as much as I did him, and I finally got it. He can be so demanding, but just a single touch from him tells me that I mean so much more than just a fling.

I move around the front of my sex-romped bed and feel satisfied shivers run through me. Looking at him sound asleep and handsomely naked, I realize he's in the spot I always felt he belonged.

People say that childhood dreams never really come true, but mine has. For once in my life, I'm getting something I really want, and he wants me in return. Cloud nine it's nice to meet you finally.

I look down at my very own naked body and quickly try to find something to throw on. Only successfully finding his shirt from last night, I throw it on and button it up. It comes down to about mid-thigh on me, and I have to roll up the sleeves. After buttoning up a few, I grab the collar and take in Cade's scent. I hate to have to wash it off my body because it feels right having it all over me.

I smile down at Cade as he rolls over to his side to face the side of the bed I just jumped out of. He looks so sweet even when he lets out a snore. I walk over to the side and give him a kiss on the cheek before I walk into the bathroom to do my morning business.

My God! I look like shit! My hair is flying everywhere and my make-up from last night makes me look like a crazy killer clown. Quickly, I run a brush through my hair and toss it up in a messy bun then clean my face.

I yawn again when I walk out of the bathroom back into my room. "Now that's one sexy sight." I open my eyes to see Cade lying back against my log headboard with my camouflage sheets bunched around his waist leaving his chest bare. I move from his amazing chest up to his face; he's wearing a lopsided grin. "Morning, beautiful."

"Morning." I stretch again as I make my way back to the bed.

"Now, this is the sight that I am going to love to see every morning." He wiggles his eyebrows at me as I crawl up to straddle his legs.

"What makes you think this will happen every morning?" I walk my fingers up his chest until I wrap them around his neck and smile at him.

"Because." He pulls my face to his. "I plan on waking up right here from now on." He leans down and kisses me quickly. "Deal with it, baby." He grabs a hold of my hips bringing my body flush against him.

"Cade." I giggle. Yeah, I can be a girl some times. "I have to get up."

"Why?" he asks into my neck as he kisses it.

"I have to get stuff ready to head up the mountain tomorrow." I laugh.

"Why?"

"Because Steven needs me to take food up to him, and I want to check on the cattle we have up there." I laugh as I push him away. Steven is my cousin; he is also my only hired hand. He is someone who prefers to be alone, so sending him up the mountain each summer with some of my cattle is okay with him.

He sticks his bottom lip out and starts to pout. Pouting Cade is sexy. I move to climb off him and head over to my dresser. "You can come with me if you want." I look over my shoulder and wink. "I'm actually thinking of sending Steven down for a couple days and stay up there myself until he comes back."

That cheered him right up. "You and me at the cabin by ourselves for a couple days?" He grins and nods. "I like the sound of that."

"Cade ... I'm going up there ... to ..." Words die when he stands up and the sheets fall from his waist relieving his very naked and happy body. *Oh Lord, that was in me? Wow, I'm one lucky girl.*

"Like what ya see, sugar?" He walks up to me, kisses my cheek then moves into the bathroom.

"Work! I'm going up there to work!" I shake my thoughts back. He laughs as he comes back out buttoning his pants up.

He stops in front of me and kisses my forehead. "We will work, but at night we can have some fun." He starts to walk out of my room. Once the door is open, Timber comes flying in yipping her head off. It is bathroom time for her. "I'll go pack a bag," he offers then disappears.

Shaking my head, I look down at Timber. "Need to go potty, baby girl?" She yips up at me. "Okay. Let's go." She follows me out of the room and down to the door.

~*~*~*~

I LAUGH FOR the millionth time since walking into the grocery store with Cade. Seeing this overgrown, muscle-bound cowboy pushing a shopping cart is a funny sight.

I'm really enjoying the sight from behind, too. *Yes, I'm ogling his ass.*

"What else do we need, Emma?" Cade looks over his shoulder at me and then shakes his head when he catches me looking at his ass...again. "Next time, you push the damn cart." He starts to walk off.

"Yeah, well, learn a lesson from stealing it from me." I stomp after him. I walk past him toward the milk and eggs. "We'll need to take fresh milk, eggs, and orange juice up there. It's been a couple weeks since I took groceries."

I bend over to look through the egg cartons, earning a whistle from Cade. Rolling my eyes, I open one to check the eggs. One should always check their eggs before purchasing them. Never know, one time you may not, and then go to open them and BAM dead baby chick inside. It's happened before.

"Oh! My! Gawd!" I shoot straight up with an instant glare on my face. I turn around to see Lilly making her way over to Cade and me. Well, Cade, since he's blocking her view of me. "Cade Masters?" her high-pitched nasal voice calls.

Cade turns to see who is talking to him with a frown in place.

Eggs forgotten, I walk around him and loop my arm in one of his, causing Lilly to stop in her tracks. "Emma?" She gives me a disgusted look before turning her fake-ass smile on Cade and pretending that I'm not even standing there. "Been a long time." She flirts with him. *I want to throw up.*

My Cowboy

"Yeah." He leans back a bit as she steps closer to him.

"Lilly?" Right on cue, Trey walks around the corner pushing a cart with Lilly's purse in it. "Oh...hey, Emma." He smiles at me, and I glare. He looks up and sees Cade next to me and my arm in his. "Cade?" He's shocked to see him.

Obviously, these two weren't at the rodeo, which is hard to believe. Lilly is a bona fide buckle bunny, and Trey is a wannabe cowboy.

"Hey, Trey." Cade nods at him and turns back to look at the eggs.

"So...you're back in town for good, Cade?" I cannot believe...no wait, I can believe that she is still flirting with Cade, who shows more interest in the eggs than her and right in front of her boyfriend.

"Yeah. Emma and I are trying to get the Price Ranch back on its feet," he mutters as he puts some eggs in the cart and starts pushing it away.

"Well, maybe we could get together sometime?" *She's actually twirling her damn hair!*

Cade turns and gives a quick smile before grabbing my hand. "Don't think so. My girl wouldn't like that, and I don't think your boyfriend would be too happy."

A stupid goofy-ass grin comes across my face as she looks dumbstruck from the letdown. "HA!" I let out as we walk off.

"Thank you." I smile up at Cade after we stop in front of a checkout.

"You're welcome." He grins at me before leaning down to place a sweet kiss on my lips. "Don't need you fighting in the grocery store."

I start to unload the cart. "Wouldn't be the first time."

"God, you're feisty!" He throws back his head and laughs.

~*~*~*~

LATER THAT NIGHT, everything that doesn't need to be keep cold has been packed into the back of my truck. We have brought in Scooter, as well as Ripper. I'm a bit nervous about taking him, but maybe being put to work will settle him down a bit.

We are sitting on the back porch watching Timber chase some birds while we eat the ranch burgers that I just made.

"Man!" Cade swallows his bite. "It's been forever since I had one of these!"

I smile and lean over to wipe some mustard off the side of his mouth and pop my finger into my mouth. "Maybe you should've come home sooner. I basically live off of these."

"I thought about it a few times." He looks up toward the pink sky.

"Why did you wait till now?" I stare down at my half-eaten burger.

He sighs. "I didn't think I would be welcomed back. The way I left was bad. You were right, I was only thinking of myself." He grabs my hand and brings it up to his mouth to kiss it lightly.

"I love hearing those words." I smile up at him. "My parents would have been thrilled to have you back." I look out to the yard and see Timber run right into the fence post. What is wrong with that dog?

"What about you and Tucker?" I look at him from the corner of my eye and shrug.

"I don't know about Tucker, my reaction would have been the same as I did when you came back. I was really mad at you for a long time. I felt hurt and that I didn't matter to you." I lean back on my hands.

"Losing Pop really messed me up for a while. I thought if I went out on my own and proved I could do something with my life then it would fill the hole that his death left in me...I was wrong."

"How did you know you were wrong?"

My Cowboy

He sets his plate on the side and does the same with mine before turning me to face him. "Seeing you ..."

I arch a brow. "Seeing me helped how?"

He moves closer to me and takes my hands in his. "Seeing you...being near you...it heals me." He looks into my eyes, making me suck in a breath. His eyes are filled with ... love?

I shake my head. "I don't do that." I pull my hands from his. "I can't. I'm not that special." I get up, grab our plates, and start to walk into the house. "It's being home that helps, not me."

Once I get to the sink, I throw the plates in and brace myself against the counter. "You do, though." He wraps his arms around my waist and lays his head on my shoulder. "I was lost for a long time, Emma. Coming home was the best thing for me. Being with you." He squeezes me. "Like this. I can breathe again." He kisses my neck before turning me to face him.

"I'm not that special of a girl, Cade." I look down. "I'm sure you could have found someone better than me."

He lifts my chin. "No one mattered till you, Emma. Just because some other guy, a stupid idiot, couldn't see how special you are doesn't mean that you aren't."

He leans down brushing his lips lightly across mine once then sinks into a deep kiss. His hands come up as his thumbs rub my cheeks. When he pulls back, his eyes have darkened. "Let me love you." He grabs my hand leading me out of the kitchen and up to my...*our* room.

Once up to the room, he slowly undresses the both of us before coming over to pick me up and settling me in the middle of the bed.

He crawls up between my legs trailing his fingers on both on his way up. He sweetly kisses me as his fingers slowly part me and rub against my clit.

"Cade," I softly moan as he moves down and takes one of my nipples in his mouth.

"Damn, baby, you're wet." He smiles up at me then moves to my other nipple. I arch my back to bring them up closer to him and rock against his hand.

Slow and steady, he moves his fingers in and out of me till I reach my climax and sweetly moan as I play with his short soft dark brown hair. "Oh, Cade."

He smiles up at me. "Ready, baby?" I bite my lip and nod.

He moves closer to me. He kisses me as he slowly enters me. "Emma, you're my own piece of heaven, sugar." Once he's all the way in, he stays there for a minute, just long enough so we feel our connection.

He slowly rocks in and out of me, building up between us. I start to rock my hips against his to the same beat. He kisses my eyelids. "You're my perfect fit." He speeds up just a little causing my breath to catch and my head to fall back, exposing my neck.

Cade sweetly kisses both sides. "I'm getting closer, sugar."

I moan because that is all I can do. My next climax hits me sweetly like the one before. "Cade." I pull him down to kiss him and swallow his own moan as he finds his release. After we break our kiss, he smiles down at me.

"You do heal me." He kisses my nose, rolls onto his side taking me with him, and wraps his arms around me snugly. I smile into his shoulder. *This is what I always wanted.*

Chapter Nine

I STILL CANNOT manage to shake the bad feeling that I have. This morning when we loaded up my truck this feeling came over me, causing me to grab my gun before we headed out.

Since I grabbed my gun, Cade beat me to the truck to climb in the driver's seat. "I need to talk to you about something, Cade." I chance a look over at him as we wind up the mountain.

"What's up, sugar?" He looks over at me before turning back to the road.

"Well, we've had...sex and a couple of times now and haven't used protection." I play with the hem of my tank top. "I should let you know that I'm not on the pill or any other form of birth control." When he says nothing, I continue, "All the different birth controls I've tried have messed me up, and since I've been single, I haven't really worried about it..."

"Emma..." I look over at Cade and notice that he doesn't look too happy.

"What?"

He lets out a nervous laugh. "Well, first off...I've always used protection." He glances at me real quick. His eyes look so sad. "And...I can't..." His grip tightens on the steering wheel. "I can't have kids, Emma."

"Huh?" I'm puzzled; he's a healthy twenty-eight, almost twenty-nine-year-old.

Again, he lets out a nervous laugh. "The accident..."

I think for a second then it hits me. "Oh..." That's right; when he got into the accident with Nate, something stabbed him.

"Yeah. The doctors said that I probably will never have kids of my own." He pulls his shades down over his eyes.

I really don't know what to say. But I don't feel ready for this conversation, so best if I change it. "I'm amazed you remember where to go."

"Gee thanks, Emma." He smiles over at me. "Not like I didn't spend all my childhood summers up here or nothing." We both laugh.

I look out the window and see the cabin coming into view. *My own little piece of heaven.* This cabin has been in the Price family for sixty years and little has changed over the years. The only toilet is still an outhouse, only running water is in the sink, no cable, and two bedrooms. I love this place.

I used to tell Cade, Libby, and Tucker that I was going to move up here someday and live off the land. Now, the cabin works well when we bring the cattle up. Steven mainly lives in it but from time to time, someone from the family stays in it.

As we pull up, Steven comes walking out not looking too happy. "Em." He nods to me. As I finish getting out and grab my bag and gun, I frown up at him.

"What's wrong, Steven?"

He lets out a sigh and shrugs his shoulders. "We've had some kills. Yesterday morning I was up at Bull Draw and found three calves killed and ripped open. Then this morning..." He leans against the truck shaking his head. "There were three more. They were the bigger calves, too."

I open up the back end and let Timber out of her kennel. "Bull Draw?" He nods. I look over at Cade. "Unload the boys; we'll ride up once we get everything inside." He nods and goes to the trailer. I turn back to Steven. "Drive down and call Game and Fish or Wildlife Services. Preferably Game and Fish." Steven nods and heads for his truck.

~*~*~*~

My Cowboy

"WHY PERFERABLY GAME and Fish?" Cade asks as we start up a hill leading to the bedding ground in Bull Draw.

I shake my head. "Because last time I dealt with Wildlife Services, I was arrested for assault." I laugh remembering what happened two summers ago.

"What?" Cade laughs.

"Long story...Dad wasn't too happy, but Lester pissed me off so bad I just lost it."

"Wait!" I look over at Cade who is now surprised. "Lester? As in Lester Box?"

I nod. "The very same."

"The Toad! He works for Wildlife Services?" He's really laughing now.

"Watch it, cowboy, you may lose your seat." I wink at him then move Ripper around a group of trees. "He thinks he's Mister Hot Shot now. And I guess he was trying to get some form of payback for all the shit you and Tucker put him through in school."

"Through you?" His laughing calmed a little.

"Yeah." Now it's my turn to laugh. "What he didn't take into account is that I would swing at him."

"And you got arrested?"

"Yep, but the charges were dropped. The game warden, my dad, and Steven told the judge what happened and I was let off the hook." I shrug.

"Man, sugar, you really are feisty." He shakes his head then turns back to the trail. Once we reach the clearing, both horses stop. Out in the middle, I see three of the calves and farther down the draw, I see the other three. "Shit."

I nod and get off Ripper then tie him to a tree. Once I reach the first calf, I look him over. His throat has been ripped out all the way down to his lungs, which are missing. "Crap." I bend down and open up his chest. "Everything else is still here except his heart and lungs." I look up at Cade who is making his way to the next calf.

"Same with this one, Emma." He stands up, brushes off his hands, and moves to the next one.

Once we've looked over the other calves, we walk back to the horses. I stop halfway back to the horses and look down at the track in front of me. "That's too big for a coyote." Cade, who is a few feet in front of me, stops, turns, and looks down.

He touches it then looks up at me. "Wolf?"

I blink and shake my head. "Possibly; I'm not sure if there are any around this side of the state yet. But this is no bear track." I bend down next to him and examine the track. "I have a camera in my saddle bag; grab it, please." Cade nods and runs over to the horses. I get my pocketknife out and lay it next to the track to compare sizes.

I look up and around the draw. None of my cattle are anywhere near here. I can hear them down the draw closer to the cabin, but nothing is around here. No birds, deer, squirrels, or chipmunks. "Where the hell is everything?"

Cade and I take pictures of the track and of all the kills, and then head back to the cabin. I'll have to bring a four-wheeler up here to move my calves somewhere else. I won't leave them up here.

"Probably a good thing you brought your gun," Cade says as we ride back to the cabin.

~*~*~*~

"WELL, EMMA. These are bear kills," Lester's annoying voice tells me as he looks over one of my dead calves.

"Bullshit." I stomp up to the tiny fat man. "This may be August and the bears are getting ready to hibernate but no bear kills this way." I point down at my calves. "This is a dominance kill! Or at least a play kill."

Lester adjusts his glasses and glares at me. "No, they aren't, Emma."

My Cowboy

I grab my camera and thrust the track picture in his face. "They were killed by wolves, you asshat!"

"Emma." Cade steps forward, grabbing my shoulders.

"Let me see, Emma." Clint Thomas, the game warden and longtime frenemy of Tucker's, grabs the camera from me. He looks from the camera back down to my calves, then to Lester. "I think she's right, Box."

"No. No. No." The toad shakes his head. "There are no wolves up here. It's bear kills, meaning I can't do anything about it." He crosses his arms.

"You little fat bastard! They are wolf kills!" Cade's grip on my arms tightens, holding me back from beating this man again.

"Emma, calm down. I don't feel like explaining to a judge why you hit this man...again." Clint looks over at me then bends down to one of the calves. "Heart and lungs are the only parts missing." He looks back up at Lester. "If it was a bear, it would have eaten a whole hell of a lot more and..." He stands. "A bear would have killed maybe two not six."

"They could have been play kills, too." Cade loosens his grip on me. "Which still means something needs to be done."

I glare over at Lester as he adjusts his glasses again. "Well, nothing I can do." He moves back to his truck.

"Go ahead, go...piss off, toad!" I'll handle it myself. "Go figure for a government worker." He freezes for a brief second then gets in his truck and leaves. "Fuck face," I mutter as Cade finally releases me and we turn to Clint.

"Well, wolves are considered predators over here." He also moves to his truck to leave. "Sorry for your losses, Emma. If you find what did this, shoot it." He gets in and starts to leave but stops next to us. "Hey, Emma."

"Yeah." I look up at him.

"Tell Libby I had a great time the other night." He smiles and drives off.

What? Okay, Libby Nicole, I guess you aren't on a dry streak. But still, Clint? He can be nice in a professional setting, but he's an ass in a personal one.

I shake my head and plant my face in one of my hands. "Hey." Cade turns me and pulls me into his embrace. "I'll find what did this, baby." He kisses the top of my head. "I'll find it."

~*~*~*~

"EMMA." I feel a hand on my bare shoulder. "Emma, baby, wake up."

"No, go away." I bat Cade's hand away. "It's too early." I roll over and bury myself in the pillows.

"Emma. Sugar, get your ass up now." The next thing I know, Cade is hoisting me into his arms and walking out the front door.

"Cade!" I yelp and wrap my arms around his neck. I'm wide awake now. It's still dark and cool outside. "What the fuck! Let me go back to bed, you brute." I slap him on the chest. "I'll make it worth your while." I wink up at him.

"Oh, sugar, I'll make waking up worth your while," He assures as he carries me down to the truck. I look and notice the tailgate is down and Timber is on the ground in front of it growling.

"What the hell?" I wipe the sleep from my eyes as Cade puts me to the ground gently. I adjust my eyes in the darkness and notice there is something big and furry in the bed of the truck. "What is that?" I strain my eyes to see. Then Cade turns a flashlight on. "Holy shit!" I jump back into his arms.

"I told you that I would get it, sugar," he whispers into my ear. I look back at the dead wolf in the back of my truck. "There was another one, but it took off before I had time to reload."

"Holy shit." I walk closer and look it over. Male, not sure the age, about 150 pounds from the look of him and deader than a doornail. "Wow…" I'm a little shocked. I didn't even realize Cade had gotten out of bed during the night and left. I look down at

My Cowboy

Timber, who is still growling, and pick her up so she can see. "Cool your roll, baby girl." I pet her head and turn to Cade. "We'll have to call Clint and report this." I look back at the wolf. "But I want to keep his skull and pelt." I smile up at Cade and get up on my tiptoes to kiss him. "Thank you," I whisper against his lips.

"You're welcome, baby." He kisses me again then shuts the tailgate before picking me up again. "Now, what's this about making it worth my while?"

I giggle as he carries me into the cabin. "Let me put Timber down and I'll show you how grateful I am, cowboy."

As Cade sets me on the couch, Timber jumps out of my arms and runs back toward the closed door, continuing to bark at the dead wolf. Cade shakes his head at her and laughs. "What an odd dog."

"You have no idea." I grab him and pull him down next to me. I move over the top of him and slowly remove my nightshirt and then his shirt. "Thank you for avenging my calves."

"You're welcome." His voice has gotten thick with lust as I move to undo his pants and slide them down his legs. "Emma...sugar...you don't need to..."

"Bullshit." I glare up at him. "Let me take care of you." I move to his boxer briefs and notice that I'm not the only one excited.

I bring his boxer briefs down, lick my lips, and smile up at him. I wrap my hand as best as I can around him and slowly start to pump him as I bring my lips down and lick him from his tip to his base.

"Fuck..." He throws his head back and jerks up a little against my mouth. I smile and bring my other hand up to massage his balls.

I swirl my tongue around his head, suck it into my mouth, bring him to the back of my throat, and swallow.

"Jesus, Emma!" He jerks up again and stares down at me with hooded eyes. I start to pump him with my hand a little faster and tightly pull my mouth back up. He grabs some of my hair and starts to slowly rock into my mouth. "Sugar, that feel s-so ... good." He draws out as I start to move faster.

I'm enjoying this control; I lightly bite his tip making him jerk against my mouth once more. "Fuck, baby!" I go back to pumping and massaging him. Soon, I feel his balls draw up. "I'm close baby." I start to move faster. "Emma. I don't ... f-f-fuck. I don't want to come in your mouth, Emma."

When I don't stop, he grabs me and hauls me up onto his lap. He makes quick work of my panties and thrusts up into my wet core. "Ooooo." I throw my head back. He starts pumping into me fast and hard causing my whole body to shake.

He pulls one of my hardened nipples into his mouth licking, sucking, and lightly biting it. "Oh, Cade!" I meet his thrusts with my own. Soon, I feel my own climax coming. "Cade, I'm coming!"

"I know, baby!" He starts to rub my clit with his thumb, throwing me over the edge.

"Cade!" I scream.

"Milk me, sugar." His thrusts become eager and uncontrolled. A few more times and he releases inside me, calling out my name.

I fall into his chest and waiting arms. He wraps me in his embrace kissing the top of my head. After our breathing calms down, I look up at him and smile. I feel it, but I'm too scared to say *I love you*. Instead, I say, "Hungry?" I smile and start to get up. "I'll make the almighty hunter something to eat."

"Naked?" He gives me a heart-melting grin.

"Sure." I wink at him and move to the kitchen area and start to get breakfast together. "Then maybe some fishing later?"

"A woman after my own heart." He starts the coffee for us. "Naked breakfast and fishing. Perfect."

My Cowboy

I laugh and bat at his arms. "I'll have clothes on for fishing, Cade...well, maybe my little camo bikini," I tease as I start the eggs.

"You're goin' to kill me, baby."

Chapter Ten

"I'LL BE JUST a minute," I tell Cade as I get out of the truck and walk into Moose Lodge to call Clint Thomas.

I pay to use the phone and wait for him to pick up. I look at the clock on the wall. *10:00 am.* He should be up.

"Hello." I frown and pull the phone away. Did I call Libby? "Hello?"

"Lib?"

"Em?" I'm still puzzled. "Emma, is that you?"

"Umm ... yeah." I shake my head. "Libby, why are you answering Clint's phone?"

She giggles. Well, there's my answer. "Why are you calling him?"

"Who's that on the phone, babe?" *Babe, really?*

Libby giggles again and tells Clint it's me. "Emma, what is it that you need, my dear?" she coos into the phone. *Okay, what has happened to my best friend? She never lets a guy get to her like this.*

"I need Game Warden Thomas to get his butt back up here."

I hear some shuffling and then Clint talks. "What's going on, Emma?" He's all business now. *Poor, poor Libby.*

"Cade killed a wolf that was going after my calves again early this morning."

"Okay. I'll be up as soon as I can."

"I get to keep the fucker, don't I?"

"Yeah...I just need blood samples to see if I can find out where it came from. I just need to look it over."

"Okay good, because I'm mounting the bastard in my living room."

He laughs. "Okay. I'll be up there as soon as I can."

"Thank you, Warden." I laugh.

"Welcome, Emma."

After I hang up, I head back out to the truck. "So?"

I look over at Cade and smile. "He'll be up after a while. So, you want to hit a fishing spot close to the cabin?"

He grins. "Our secret spot?"

I laugh. "You remembered!"

"Of course. That was the best fishing spot. Plus..." He throws the truck and reverse and we take off. "We can see anyone pulling up to the cabin from there."

~*~*~*~

"DAMMIT, EMMA! Hold still." Cade reaches over again, but I can't stop. "Emma!"

"Want it off? Work for it, honey." I move again.

"Fucking damn shit, Emma! Hold still!" Cade reaches again and this time manages to get his pole from me.

I start laughing. "Chill out, Cade. It's just a fish."

"Yeah, a huge-ass fish." I stick my tongue out at him and go back to my pole.

Like we always did in our spot, we try to see who can catch the bigger fish. So far, he's winning. "It's not about the size."

He barks a laugh. "Oh sugar, you enjoy the size." He winks over at me. We aren't talking about fish anymore.

I turn back and watch my pole bend, indicating that I got a bite. I start reeling my fish in while Cade re-baits his hook and casts off. "Holy shit! This is a big fish."

"Yeah, right." Cade walks down stream with his pole as he reels back in.

"Bullshit!" I pull my fish out of the water and just stare.

Cade makes his way back over to me and starts laughing. I mean, he is cracking up so hard he falls over. "Yeah, that's a big fish, sugar!"

I hold it up and stare at it. It's a rainbow but only about three inches long. "This tiny fucker is strong." I get him off my hook and throw him back.

Cade manages to stand up in front of me. "Don't worry, sugar; I've got a big enough fish for the both of us." He winks.

I glare up at him, shoving him into the stream. Now it's my turn to laugh. His ass planted in the muddy bottom.

As I'm laughing, I don't notice the huge clod of dirt that he picks up and throws at me. The clod smacks me right in the face, causing me to choke on some mud. "Cade, you asshole!"

He goes to stand, but I launch myself at him, throwing us back into the water and mud. I grab some mud and his hat. "Don't you dare, Em ..." I slap the mud right on the top of his head then put his hat back on. "...ma."

I turn to get away from him, but he grabs me, throws me down, and starts grabbing mud. I grab some the best I can and grip the waist of his pants. I dump some down the front, causing him to shiver and glare at me.

Next, he grabs the front of my bikini top and rubs mud all over my chest. "Fucker!"

"Get what you deserve, baby," he teases, then bends down and kisses me. It's a slow, sweet kiss that takes my breath away.

When he comes back up, I smile at him. "I think we scared all the fish away."

He runs a muddy hand through his hair and laughs. "Yeah, I guess we did." He stands then helps me up.

I pat myself down and feel a really uncomfortable feeling slide down my butt. I make a face and look up at him. "I think I got

My Cowboy

mud up my butt." Turning me around, he laughs then gathers some water in his hat and dumps it down my back. "Thank you."

Once we are back on the shore, I look over at the cabin and see Clint's truck pulling up. "Fun's over. Let's go." I can see he is by himself. *Go figure. He can't even bring her along.*

Cade grabs our poles and my hand. As we make our way through the willows and toward the cabin, he suggests, "We should go out tomorrow night."

"What, like a date?" I smile up at him.

"Yeah, a date." He kisses my forehead. "We haven't yet and I feel I should."

"Okay." I laugh to myself. "Not to sound too much like a girl, but what should I wear?"

He laughs with me. "I'm glad you're a girl, baby...do you own a dress?"

I hold up a finger. "One."

"Okay, well wear that *one* dress."

~*~*~*~

I SMILE OVER the table at Cade, who is looking sexy in his black button up with clean blue Wranglers and dirty old brown Justin boots. I look down at myself. I'm in my one and only dress a strapless white sundress with my own pair of well-worn brown Ariat boots.

"You look beautiful, Emma," Cade tells me for the millionth time since I came down the stairs at the house.

"Thank you. You're lookin' pretty good, too, cowboy." I wink at him.

I curled my long straight blond hair and put my bangs up in the bump thing girls do. To me, I look classy. I look around the restaurant; Cade brought me to the nicest steak house in fifty miles of Elk Field. For that, I'm grateful.

We've both already ordered our meals. He complained about how I like my steak, again.

"Some things never change." He shook his head as he handed the waiter his menu.

"I can't stand blood or any pink in my steak. I never plan on changing that about me." I stuck my tongue out at him.

He laughed.

"So, tell me, Mr. Masters." I bring my hands up to reach a peak in front of me. "Who's captured your heart in the past?"

He leans forward and rests his elbows on the table. "No one really. There have been girls, but none who meant much till recently."

"Oh really?" I smile at him. "Anyone I know?"

He bites his bottom lip then sits back shaking his head. "Probably not. You see this girl is a hard ass and a big tomboy. Looking at your lovely self, I don't think you two would ever meet."

My smile grows. "I may surprise you. I may look nice." I gesture to my dress. "But I know how to get dirty and I'm not afraid to." I take a drink of my water.

"Oh. I don't doubt that." He winks back at me.

"So, really. Seriously, no girl?"

"None. I was always on the move and never took the time to settle." He shrugs. "Now, what about you?"

"Oh…well, there have been a few guys, but none who had my heart. That's been off-limits for a long time."

"Not even one?"

"Well … there was … one." I narrow my eyes and hold up a single finger.

"Who?" He's smiling and leaning forward again.

"As if you have to ask." Continuing to smile he just waits. "You, you moron." I take another drink and look away.

"How old were you when you first felt something for me?" He's amused; well, I'm glad my childhood crush is amusing.

I turn and look him straight in the eye. "Ten. I was ten; you were fourteen."

"How did your crush develop?"

"You're finding this amusing, aren't you?"

"Of course."

I sigh. "We were in the barn helping Springer get her colt out. Dad's arm was broken and you had to step in and pull him out."

"That's what did it?"

"Yeah, you were strong and you saved the colt that would have probably died." I shrugged.

He smiles at me. "Well, most girls are won over by some romantic act, and my girl just happens to be won over by a colt being born."

I lean forward. "I like being your girl."

"I like you being my girl, too."

~*~*~*~

THE REST OF dinner was wonderful; I really don't know what else to say about it. I cuddle up next to Cade in his truck as we drive down the driveway.

I would have never imagined we would be at this point. I'm thrilled that we are. I feel like I'm on cloud nine.

Once we park, we get out, walking hand in hand up to the house, and I stop in my tracks. Maddi is sitting on our steps.

"Maddi?" I let go of Cade's hand and walk up to her.

She looks up at me with tears in her eyes. "Hi, Emma," she says weakly.

Chapter Eleven

"OH, GOD." I rush over and hug her. "Maddi, what happened? Tucker ... he's not ..."

"No. No." She wipes her eyes, but the tears continue to fall. "That jackass is fine."

I let go of her. "What happened, Maddi?"

She lets out the saddest sigh I've ever heard. "He was with Faith Preston," she huffs.

"What!" I jump up and plant my hands on my hips.

"I know." She starts crying again.

"When!" I'm pissed at that idiot brother of mine. He has an amazing woman waiting for him. He needs to pull his head out of his ass, and he goes after some other one! I feel Cade's hands on my shoulders as if trying to calm me.

I brush them off and wait for Maddi's answer. "This last weekend. But I found out tonight before I got off work." She continues to cry.

I sit back down and wrap my arms around her as she continues to tell me. "She came walking in bragging about it. I couldn't even finish my shift, so I left. He called, said he wanted to talk, and I told him to go to hell. Then threw my phone out the window and headed here." She buries her face in my shoulder.

"Bastard." I continue to hold her but look up to see headlights heading our way.

Tucker gets out of his truck and makes his way over to us. Once he is standing next to Cade he thrusts his hands into his pockets. "God, Maddi, Angel, tell me what's..."

My Cowboy

I storm up to my big brother and point him in the chest. "Get your shit together, Tucker!" I turn around and gesture at Maddi to stand. "This amazing woman has been patient and waited and waited for you to get your shit together and all you fucking do is rip her heart out!"

"Emma, calm down, baby." Cade tries to come up to me. "I'm sure he can explain what happened." He looks over his shoulder at Tucker, who nods.

"Fuck that shit!" I rip my truck keys out of Cade's hands. "Don't you dare defend the bastard."

"Emma ..."

"No, Cade!" I turn and glare up at him. "What he did was wrong!" I look over at Tucker. "What the hell is wrong with you?"

I get Maddi into the passenger seat of my truck and walk around to my side. Cade grabs me to hug me. "Back off, Cade!" I shove out of his arms and get into the driver's seat. "If you think he can explain how his dick accidentally got into another woman then fuck you!" I peel out of the driveway and head toward town.

~*~*~*~

MADDI CONTINUES TO cry as I drive. I'm taking her home, and hopefully, Tucker won't follow. *What in the hell is wrong with my brother? I know he loves Maddi, but what is he trying to prove?*

Can't he see that Maddi loves him with all her heart? If she didn't, she wouldn't have stayed around here waiting for him to come back to her.

"I've lost him, haven't I, Emma?" Her broken voice carries through the cab.

I shake my head. "No, he lost you." I grit my teeth and pound on the steering wheel. "What the fuck is wrong with him!"

Maddi remains quiet till we get to the house. "Emma, I don't want to be here."

"What, you want to head back home to your parents?"

Her head shoots up at me. "God, no! I still love him no matter what Emma. I just..." She looks back down. *She has more strength in Tucker than I do.*

"Don't want to be here." She nods. "Well, I know where we can go." I put the truck back in drive. I'm glad Libby is working tonight.

~*~*~*~

GETTING LOST IN the music coming through the speakers relaxes me more than the beer running through my veins, even though I've only had two. Maddi, on the other hand, has lost herself in whatever Libby is willing to give her.

She's stripped off her work clothes and changed into some back-up clothes that were in my truck.

I stop dancing and look over at the bar where Clint is flirting with Libby, who is all googly eyed at him. *Very non-Libby.*

Shaking my head, I turn back to Maddi, who seems to be doing more of a striptease than dancing anymore. "Whoa there, girl." I grab her and drag her back to the bar. "Let's sit for a while."

"I want to be free, Emma!" She spins in a circle then plops into her seat falling into Clint's side.

He shakes his head and leans across the bar, giving Libby a very non-PG kiss, then leaves.

I look over at her. "Wowza! Go Libby!"

"Shut it!" She blushes...Libby Jones actually blushes! Then she comes back to the same Libby I know and love. "I give good vagina hugs." She shrugs and moves down the bar to refill some drinks.

Maddi starts laughing. "I thought I did, too," she pouts. *What has my brother done to this sweet girl?*

I roll my eyes and go back to my second beer. "You know he just dumped his fiancée for bullshit reasons right?" Libby just stares. I shake my head. "I just don't want to see you get hurt, Lib."

My Cowboy

"I'm a big girl, Em. I'll be fine." She storms down the bar to take care of another customer.

As pissed as I am, a beer or any liquor isn't doing it for me tonight. I don't feel the greatest.

An hour later, Maddi has been to the bathroom twice to throw up but hasn't stopped drinking. Little does she know, Libby is watering down her drinks. I gave up on beer and went for water even though I'm feeling even worse now. My head is light and my vision is freaking out on me.

As I'm taking a drink ,I feel a hand touch my shoulder and start to turn me. I was thinking Tucker, but I was dead wrong.

"Hey, Emma." His grin, which used to be cute, now just looks creepy.

"Trey." I turn back toward the bar. "Where's the whore?"

He takes a seat next to me and moves too close. "I don't know." He looks me up and down. "What's the special occasion that has you so dressed up?"

I arch a brow at him. "Go away, Trey." I turn to look away and shake my head as my vision blurs.

"Come on, E. We were great together." He turns me again.

"No, we weren't." He grabs my shoulders and forces me to look at him.

"Come on. Come back to me, sweetie." I hate being called sweetie, unless it's from my mom.

"No." I go to stand but fall back down and grab my head. Black dots come to my eyes and I can't seem to shake them.

"I'll take care of you, Emma." He moves his mouth close to my ear.

"Fuck off, Trey." I push him away as best I can, but it's no good. I have no strength.

"Oh, Emma." He tries to lean in to kiss me then I feel him move away. *Thank you!*

"Leave her alone, Barker." Justin's voice booms over the sound of the music. I can't really see and my stomach is in knots.

"She can take care of herself, Foster." Trey's voice is pissed. *Oh no, don't swing at him, Trey, you'll only piss him off.*

I hear a crack of something and something falls to the ground. I can only guess...Trey. Then I feel Justin wrap an arm around my waist to help me up.

"Let's get you home, Emma."

I nod. "I don't feel good."

"Hate to be blunt, Emma, but you look like shit."

"Thanks," I mutter. "Wait! Get Maddi. She needs to go home, too."

"Okay. But let me get you to my truck first." He carries me out and into his truck then goes back in for Maddi. *Why can't Libby go for Justin? He may get around, but so does she. He would be good to her and only her.*

I feel someone carrying me up some stairs. I try to open my eyes, but when I do I can't really see anything so I close them again and groan.

"What the fuck happened!" I hear Cade as the front door opens.

"She was at the bar. She didn't look too good, so I decided to get her home." Justin gets us in the front door and makes his way to my room.

"How much did she drink?" Cade's voice is close and filled with concern.

"Libby said she didn't drink much, only a couple." He opens my door and then lays me on my bed. "She mainly drank water, but she has no color."

"What the fuck?" Someone sits on the bed next to me and presses their hand to my forehead...Cade. "She's burning up." He gets up and I hear the water run in the bathroom then something cold on my forehead. "Thank you, Justin. For bringing her home."

"No problem." They both start to leave. "Take good care of her, Cade, she's pretty special."

"I fully plan on it." I hear them go downstairs. I try to get up and take my boots off at least, but it's too hard. "Emma!" Cade runs over to me. "Lay down, baby."

"My boots." I groan and lay back down.

"I got 'em." He pulls each of my boots off.

"Cold, Cade," I whine and blindly reach for him.

I feel his arms wrap around me as he lies down next to me. I feel comfortable for now. "I'm sorry, Cade."

He kisses the side of my neck. "It's okay, sugar. It's okay."

Chapter Twelve

I WAKE WITH a jolt and rush to the bathroom, barely making it to the toilet. "Fuck," I groan after I empty my stomach. I wipe my forehead and look up to see Cade standing at the door. "How do you feel?"

He shrugs. "Fine, why?" He leans against the door.

"I don't think dinner agreed with me last night." I slowly get up and move to wash my face and brush my teeth.

He walks up to me and presses his lips to my forehead. "You don't feel hot anymore." He takes my face in his hands and turns me to look at him. "How do you feel now?"

Shrugging and pulling the toothbrush from my mouth. "Fine, my stomach hurts like hell." I bend down, go to spit, and nearly throw up again. "Fuck." I lay my head on the edge of the sink and shake it.

Cade rubs his hand up and down my back. "Maybe you should stay in bed today."

"I can't." I look up at him through my hair. "I need to bring in calves to ship." I stand back, lay my head against his bare chest, and play with the small patch of hair.

"I'll handle it." He continues to rub my back and kisses my forehead. "Go back to bed. I'll call Tucker and see if he can come out and help on one of the four-wheelers."

"I'm fine, Cade." I move past him to change my clothes as I'm still in my dress from last night. I stumble and lean against the bedpost.

My Cowboy

"You are not." Cade marches up to me and picks me up. "Go back to bed, it's still really early." He lays me down and covers me back up. "I'll bring you some crackers and something to drink."

I start to sit up, but he pushes be back down. "I mean it, Emma."

I cross my arms and glare at him. "Fine." Pouting, I turn away from him and look out at the darkened sky through my window.

"Good girl." He kisses my cheek and leaves the room.

~*~*~*~

I STRETCH AND roll to my side to check the time. *1:45 pm.* Shit, I slept a long time. I sit up to stretch, and notice the items next to my clock on my side of the bed. He brought me club crackers and some water. *How sweet.* I smile and reach for them.

Before I fell back asleep, I changed into a sports bra and my yoga pants, even though I don't do yoga. My stomach still hurts, but that might be because I woke up a couple more times to throw up.

It feels a little weird waking up this late and not having Timber following me around. Plus, it is way too quiet.

Walking downstairs, I look out the front door window and see Tucker's truck parked by mine. *How in the hell did that get back here?*

"Hello. Hello, sleepy head!" There's my answer. Libby comes walking out of the kitchen with a bowl of soup. "I was just going to bring you some chicken noodle soup." She is way too bubbly.

"Morn...afternoon, lovely." I grab the bowl from her and go to sit in the living room.

"Feeling better?" I nod. "You looked horrible last night. What happened?"

Shrugging, I continue to eat. "I'm not sure. I was fine till I got to the bar." I lay my head on her shoulder.

She pats the side of my face. "Well, you can't feel as bad as Maddi right now." I frown at her. "She drank *way* too much last night. I left an hour ago, and she still had yet to move. She's on the couch out cold. Well, she has been up only to blow chunks."

I shake my head. "My brother is a dumbass."

"This we know."

"He better make it up to her in a BIG way."

"If I was Maddi, I'd kick his ass good, and then turn him into my slave." Libby chuckles as she turns on the TV.

"Would you do that to Clint?" I gaze questionably at her from the corner of my eye.

"Not sure, probably not." She shrugs and flips to one of the country music channels. "It's just fun with him, Emma."

Once the soup settles into my stomach, I lay against Libby. "We should all make a weekend of it on the mountain."

"Camping?"

"Yeah. Well, first I need to ship my calves that are up there, but afterwards, we could go to one of the lakes, fish, and hike, maybe have a cozy couple nights in tents?" I grin up at her.

"Sorry, girlie, we both have men now. I'm getting cozy in my own damn tent with my man." She giggles. *What has become of my best friend?*

"Sounds good to me. I could use some cuddle time with my cowboy." I stand up and stretch again. I'm doing this a lot for some odd reason; it feels amazing, though. "Maybe we could get Maddi and Tucker in their own tent," I throw over my shoulder.

"Perfect!" Libby jumps up and bounces around.

~*~*~*~

FRIDAY, CADE AND I drive up the mountain and load all my calves in the trucks to be shipped. I then send Steven down with the horses, and Cade and I take off for Shelly Reservoir to meet the others.

My Cowboy

When we arrive, the tents and fire pit are already set up and a fire is going. "How many calves?" Tucker asks as he carries burgers over to Maddi and Libby to cook.

"Close to a hundred and fifty." I look from him and Maddi. He sits next to her, but she is refusing to look at him. Then I look at Libby, who shakes her head and turns her attention to Clint.

"Why are you making so many burgers?" Cade asks as he comes up behind me after putting our stuff in our tent. He wraps his arms around me and I instantly want to melt into him, wishing everyone was gone.

"Justin is joining us," Tucker grumbles, and Clint looks pissed. *Why? What in the hell did Justin do to anyone; he's a great guy.*

"Who invited *him*?" Cade asks. *Again, what the hell?*

"I did." I look down at Libby. "He's in town for a while longer before he heads to the next rodeo. I thought he could use some time with friends." She gets up and walks over to her tent. This makes me smile.

"Well, I, for one, think it's nice. He's always been a good friend." I glare up at Cade. "Especially after how he helped Maddi and I out the other night. Especially me."

"Bringin' your sick ass home isn't a saint's job," Tucker mutters. He moves closer to Maddi when he sees that she is starting to shiver, but she pulls away and walks to her tent to get a coat. I shiver a little as well. For the beginning of August, it's cool out.

"He didn't just bring us home." I sit on the log in front of Cade. He follows and wraps his arms around me. "He knocked out Trey when he didn't take the hint that I wasn't leaving with him." Cade's arms go stiff around me.

"When were you going to tell me this?" he whispers in my ear.

"I just did." I look at him from the corner of my eye. "It's no big deal. I would have taken care of him by myself if Justin didn't."

Cade grumbles about something, and I decide to ignore him.

"Shit!" Libby startles us all. "Sorry. I didn't tell him to bring a tent." She looks at Tucker and Maddi. "Tucker, would you share with him?"

"Fuck, no!" He crosses his arms and goes back to playing with the fire.

"Well, then I guess he can bunk with Maddi..." I see the evil mastermind glint in her eyes. I know exactly what she is doing. *Little shit.*

Tucker jolts up. "FUCK NO!" He pulls Maddi closer to him, who is shocked and bright red. *Oh, our shy little Maddi.*

"Well, where will he sleep?" Libby tries to play innocent, which makes me laugh. She purposely didn't tell Justin to bring a tent.

"I guess...umm." Tucker looks into Maddi's eyes. "We could share a...tent?" He gives a nervous grin.

I'm trying my best to hold back a smile and laugh. I turn into Cade's neck to let it out. Hmmm...Cade smells so good.

"You okay, sugar?" I just nod.

When the burgers are almost done, Justin pulls up in his truck. "Hey guys!" He smiles down at us. I move closer to Cade so Justin has more room to sit with all of us.

"Be nice, he's my friend," I whisper as a warning into Cade's ear as I kiss his neck.

"Has he seen you naked?" *What!*

"What? No, he hasn't." I kiss right under his ear.

"Then he's good in my books." His sexy husky voice makes me bite my lip and I force my hormones to get under control so I don't drag him into the tent and ride him hard.

My Cowboy

Which is exactly what I did when we all went to bed.
~*~*~*~

THE NEXT MORNING, while the guys fish, the girls and I decide to take a hike and spend some time together.

"How was last night, Maddi?" I walk around another tree and look up at her.

She gives me a weak smile. "Well, after you and Cade decided to *go to sleep,* I went to bed as well." She moves around me. "I was asleep by the time he came in."

I look at Libby, who looks as sad as me. "You know what!" Libby perks up and bounces up to us. "We should do a girls' day."

I laugh. "What do you think we are doing right now?"

She shakes her head. "I mean an actual girls' day! You know shopping, getting pretty, good food, you know?"

"Nope, not I." I smile and shake my head.

"Bullshit!" Libby cocks her hip out and plants her hands on them. "We," she points to the three of us, "are going to go to Billings, shop till we drop, and get this girl," she throws an arm around Maddi, "looking so sexy that Tucker will be crawling on his hands and knees to get her back."

"I don't …"

"I agree." I cut off Maddi. "We need to make Tucker suffer." I grab her hair. "Maybe a haircut, some color, and some sexy clothes?" I look at Libby, who is extremely giddy now. "And…I can look for a birthday present for Cade." I grin and start walking again.

"YAY!" Libby bounces behind me, grabbing Maddi and dragging her along. "We need to get you out of your shell, Miss Barnett. We need to get that girl who you were the other night out and about."

"You two are going to kill me," Maddi groans.

"Quit complaining. It will be good for the three of us." I stop in the upcoming clearing. "Libby probably needs to restock her kinky shit for Clint."

"You know it!" We all let out a little giggle.

~*~*~*~

"REMEMBER THE TIME we couldn't get them to go to sleep because they were scared Big Foot would get them?" Tucker laughs as he roasts another marshmallow.

Cade chuckles. "Yeah and they crawled in bed with us because of it." He winks down at me.

"He's real!" I yell at him, making everyone else laugh. "Seriously! He is!" I look around at everyone like some crazy woman. "Lib, back me up here!"

She only shakes her head at me as Clint wraps his arms around her.

"You bitch." I laugh at her making her stick her tongue out at me.

"Sugar, Big Foot is not real." Cade laughs as he wraps his arms around my waist, pulling me between his legs, and kisses my cheek. "But I do know something that is big and real," he whispers into my ear, making me wiggle. "Don't do that." He grits his teeth.

"What ya going to do about it?" I lick my bottom lip and look up into his heated eyes.

"Bedtime!" Cade hoists me into his arms and marches us to the tent making me giggle.

"Cade, my brother is right here."

"So, you're an adult. Deal with it, baby. He will, too." He leans in lightly and brushes his lips across mine before I pull him closer, forcing his mouth open. My tongue enters his mouth and explores the mouth I love.

Once I get a groan from him, I pull back. "What do you want for your birthday?"

My Cowboy

He grins. "I have everything that I ever need right here." He lifts me again then enters our tent where he throws me down on the sleeping bag.

"Oh, you're so sweet." I move onto my knees and start to undo his pants. "Let's make you a little dirty now."

"Do your worse, sugar." He pulls his hat, hoodie, and shirt off all at once.

Once I have him naked in front of me, he pushes me down and starts stripping me.

"No striptease tonight?" I wiggle a little.

"No. I need you too badly." Once I'm naked, he kisses down my body and settles between my legs. "You need to be quiet, baby."

I just nod as he brings his face down to my core.

I nearly bite a hole through my lip from the first pass of his tongue over my clit. I roll my eyes into the back of my head and arch my back.

He brings his fingers up into my core while sucking my clit into his mouth and lightly biting down. "Cade." I breathe.

He moves his fingers around until he finds my spot. "Fuck," I whisper, loudly. I feel him grin against me then goes back to licking me as his fingers move in and out of me.

He speeds up his movements until I topple over the edge. I try my best not to yell, but I do moan rather loudly.

"Be quiet in there!" Libby laughs.

"Fuck." I blush big time grabbing a pillow to cover my face.

Cade crawls up my body and pulls the pillow away. He's smiling. "I told you to be quiet." He laughs then stops.

I feel his head push past my entrance as he eases into me. "Be quiet, Emma. Bite me if you need to, baby."

I nod and arch my back off the ground until I feel his rock hard body against my stomach.

"You're so soft, sugar. I love being buried inside you." He slowly pulls out then rapidly thrusts into me. I groan and bite my lip again. "Don't bruise your lip, baby." He comes down and kisses me sweetly as he continues to pump in and out of me.

As he starts to pick up speed, I find it really hard to control myself. I meet his thrusts with my own and soon find my teeth in his shoulder making him start to get loud.

"Quiet in there! I'm trying to enjoy my man here!" Libby yells from where I'm guessing is her tent.

"You better not be doing anything to my sister, Masters!" Tucker yells.

Cade and I stop horrified. "I'm respecting her!" Cade yells almost crying.

I try not to laugh. "Respect me, Cade!" I yell. I hear something hard hit a tree close to our tent. I giggle. "Disrespect me, cowboy," I whisper to him as I kiss the corner of his mouth.

He starts pounding into me again, and soon I find myself falling again.

After my third climax, Cade's movements become crazy, causing me to dig my fingernails into his back and sink my teeth into his shoulder. "Fuck, baby!" He slams into me one last time finding his release.

Slowly, I pry my teeth away from him and smile. "Well, besides the interruption, that was pretty hot," I whisper breathlessly.

He pulls out and away from me. "Well, you did dirty me up." He laughs and tenderly kisses my forehead.

"That I did." I grab the shirt he had taken off and pulled it over my head. I looked at his neck and see my bite mark already starting to bruise. "Shit."

He tries to look at it then gives me a panty-melting grin. "I'll wear it with pride." He crawls into the sleeping bag, pulling me

My Cowboy

in with him. "Because my girl gave it to me." He kisses me sweetly once more before falling asleep.

Chapter Thirteen

<u>The next weekend...</u>
"SO, WHAT'S THE game plan?" Maddi asks as she drives us up to Billings in her car.

"Well ..." Libby looks in the backseat at me and grins.

I cut her off in a rush. "I need to get Cade a birthday present."

Maddi looks in the rearview mirror. "What were you planning on getting him?"

"I was thinking some ammo or maybe a coyote call. He's been going out in the mornings and calling. Since Dad passed, I haven't had the time to trap."

I look at Libby, who has a horrified expression of disgust on her face. "Fuck that shit! You need to get him something sexy."

"Why? Have a points card to fill at your favorite store?" I tease Libby.

"Yes, I do!" she huffs and turns back to the road. After a couple more minutes, she yells, "I see Billings first!" I laugh and shake my head. We use to play that game all the time when we were little. We always managed to fool the boys into looking out the side windows then we would try to beat the other. I gave up years ago.

"We need to give Maddi a makeover."

"Well, we can do that, too." Libby gets her evil smirk going. "Just think of what Tucker will do when I *accidentally* say something about Maddi having a vibrator."

"Libby!" Maddi swerves a little.

My Cowboy

I grab my oh-shit handle and glare at the both of them. "Knock it off, Libby! Let the poor girl drive."

She turns back and starts to pout. "Well, fine, but we are going there whether either of you like it or not." The evil smirk returns. "But Cade would flip if you gave him a *special* birthday present when it's just the two of you. They make stuff in camo."

"Well...I have been thinking of getting something sexy to wear." I grit my teeth and see the light come back to Libby's eyes.

"YAY!" she cheers.

"But ..."

"Crap."

"We are going to my shops first, then getting Maddi dolled up, and finally we will go to where you want to go."

"Party pooper."

~*~*~*~

I'M LOOKING THROUGH some coyote calls when my phone rings. *Cade*.

"How's it going, sugar?"

"Oh." I move the phone between my ear and shoulder. "It's going. Looking for a birthday present for you right now."

"Where ya at?" I can tell he's smiling.

"Not telling." Right as I say that the loud-speakers come on and announce a sale on arrows.

"I know where."

"Well, it doesn't matter because you'll never guess what I'm looking at." I smile and grab the one I was looking for. The kind my dad used to use.

He laughs. "What else are you girls doing today?"

"Getting Maddi some new clothes and her hair done. Then we are going to go eat somewhere then Libby has some shopping she needs to do."

"What kind of shopping?"

"You don't want to know," I mumble as I make my way over to clothes where my girls are. "What are you up to?"

He laughs again. "Pushin' cows. Since we are going to be bringing down the rest of the herd on the mountain, I decided to move the others into a different pasture...that's okay, isn't it?"

"That's fine. I was thinking the same thing." I find the girls. "Be careful, okay? I don't need to come home to find out you got yourself hurt."

"Baby, I'm tough. Don't worry."

"I'll try not to."

"Oh, before we hang up there is something I want to talk to you about soon."

"What is it?" I frown.

"Not now. When you get home, we'll talk. It's just something I've been thinking of."

"O...okay."

"It's nothing bad, Emma."

"All right, we'll talk when I get home." I smile.

"'Kay, have fun, sugar. Bye."

"Bye." I hang up the phone feeling a little sad. I wanted to hear the three little words... I snap out of it and look at the girls. "Got what I need. Ready to head to the mall?"

~*~*~*~

"I DON'T KNOW." Maddi looks from side to side in the mirror in front of her. She frowns up at me. We had the hairstylist add some highlights and hair extensions to Maddi's already beautiful head of hair. Her milk chocolate brown hair now has dirty blond highlights to it.

"Oh, shut up." I slap her shoulder. "You look great!"

She gives me a weak smile.

Libby, who has been quiet for the last hour, is starting to worry me. She's been texting I can only guess to be Clint while Maddi is having her hair colored. "Lib, you okay?"

My Cowboy

She looks up from her phone. "I want to get a piercing." Blunt as ever.

"Okay." I question her with my stare. "Where?"

I'm not sure I want the answer. "My tongue." She stands and walks over to the part of the salon where people can get piercings at. "You two should get something, too."

I laugh, and Maddi looks down. "Okay." Maddi's quiet answer startles me.

"Really!?!" Libby smiles at her.

"Yeah, I mean we are here for a makeover, so why not?"

I finally pull out of my shock. "Where?"

Maddi smiles at me and bites her lip. "My nose."

"Oh, Tucker will looove that." I roll my eyes. Maddi gets a hurt expression. "But if that's what you want ... go for it." She smiles and makes her way over to Libby.

They both stare at me waiting for me to join in. "You guys go ahead, having my ears pierced is good enough for me." I smile and walk toward them to wait for everyone to get done.

Libby decides to go first. She stand perfectly still with her tongue hanging out. Oddly, to me it reminds me of times when Timber begs. I laugh and watch in shock as Libby barely moves as the lady pierces her tongue. After she cleans it up, she explains how to take care of it and that she should be able to change the barbell looking thing in about a month.

I walk away when it is Maddi's turn. I don't think I can handle seeing what they do to pierce a nose. I walk outside and wander around the corner and see a tattoo parlor. Curiosity gets the better of me, and I walk in.

It is quiet. No one is in there except a lady at the counter. "Can I help you?"

"Oh, just looking at the moment. Thank you." I smile and turn back to the books on the table. I've always wanted a tattoo but never took the time to get one. I admire Cade's. He has a tribal band wrapped around his right bicep. I discovered a bucking bull and rider hidden in it. Made me feel good knowing that I'm the only person to find it.

On his left arm, he has a deer skull with his dad's name wrapped around it.

I flip through the pages when I get a text from Libby.

Libby: Where the hell are you?!?
Me: Next door in the tattoo parlor.
Libby: OMG! Are you going to get one?
Me: Thinking about it...
Libby: On our way!

Two seconds later, they both come in. Maddi starts looking around, and Libby marches up to me with a huge grin. "Get something. Please."

I turn the page and see a picture of a lady's back. On each shoulder blade, she has a small angel wing and at the base of her neck is a halo. The second I saw it, I wanted it. *For my dad.*

I smile, get up, and walk over to the lady at the counter. "How long would this take?" I point to the picture.

She looks it over. "Turn around." I turn and then turn back again. She looks back at the picture. "Black and white or color?"

"Black and white."

She nods. "Should only take a couple hours." She then gets a book out. "I have an opening in two hours. Want to come back then?"

I smile and nod. "Yes, please."

"Name."

"Emma Price." I give her my number just in case we can come back earlier. Just enough time to eat something.

Libby skips out to the car. "Yay! I'm so excited." Shaking my head, I get in the backseat. "Good thing my store stays open late." She winks then slides into her seat.

~*~*~*~

My Cowboy

"ALL DONE." The tattoo lady pulls back and wets a paper towel to wipe my back down. I can't believe how much that hurt. I'm glad that I didn't ask for color. I did, however, ask for her to put my dad's initials in the halo. "You can get up and take a look." She hands me a hand mirror and I move to the standing mirror.

I turn and look. "Wow." It looks amazing. My skin isn't as tan on my shoulder blades as the rest of my body, but it still looks amazing. I look at each little wing and smile. When I look at the halo nestled at the base of my neck with the initials *NHP* in the center, I feel myself start to tear up but quickly brush it off. *No crying.*

I turn back to the lady. "Thank you."

"No problem."

After I pay her, Libby starts to get super excited because she knows it's her turn to have fun.

Maddi drives nervously to the store Libby wants to visit. I think she is also having second thoughts about it because I know I am. *What will Cade think?*

"Quit worrying, you two!" Libby snaps us out of our thoughts. "The guys will go nuts," she cheers as Maddi parks the car in front of *Cat and Dog Fun House*. Seriously? What a horrible title. "Come on!"

Libby leaps out and into the store. Maddi and I exchange a nervous look and follow her in. I've never been in here before so I don't know what to expect.

There is quiet music playing through the speakers. The place is spotless, and everything is on display. Good thing they have blacked out windows.

"Come on, Maddi!" Libby pulls Maddi toward the vibrators, knowing she would be the first to back out. I follow and look at all the stuff. I have no clue what some of these things are.

I wander through the store as Libby got Maddi all set and paid for. I end up in front of the costumes. Again, curiosity gets the best of me and I start looking through them.

I stop and pull out my phone to text Cade. Hopefully, he'll have service.

Me: Do you have any sexual fantasies?

I look through some more costumes. None I really like.

Cade: What!?!

Me: You know like costumes and stuff...

Cade: Baby, are you doing Libby's shopping now?

Me: Yes.

Cade: Emma, my only fantasy is having you. I don't care what you wear or what we do. As long as it's with you, I'm good. ;)

Me: Okay.

Cade: Have fun but not too much.

Me: Be home in a couple hours.

Cade: I'll be waiting.

After sliding my phone back into my pocket, I continue to look through stuff. I pull out this little camouflage number and smile. He may not care, but I want to wear something special for him. And we both like camo so this will work.

"Good girl." I jump at the sound of Libby's voice. "Find anything else?"

"Not yet." I look over my shoulder at her. "You go do your shopping. I don't need any help." She smiles and skips off.

I go through another rack and freeze at the last costume I come to. A slow smile comes to my face. Now I know he would love this. What guy wouldn't have a fantasy about this one. I pull it out and check the size. *YES! Just my size.*

I walk over to the counter and set the fantasy costume and the camo outfit down. Libby comes over and smiles. "God, Cade is one lucky guy!" She smacks my butt and heads for the door with Maddi.

I don't know what they bought. Honestly, I don't want to know. Especially Maddi because it if she and Tucker get back together then it would more than likely mean that my brother would be using them, too. *YUCK!*

~*~*~*~

IT WAS WELL after dark when Maddi dropped me off at home. It was uncomfortable sitting the whole way down because of my tattoos. I never realized how hot and uncomfortable they would feel.

I walked into the house figuring I would be greeted by Timber and Cade, but no one was there. "Hello?" No answer. It was silent throughout the house so I carried what I bought up to the bedroom.

I hide Cade's calls and the fantasy costume I bought. Those would wait for a few weeks till his birthday. I checked again to make sure I was alone, quickly changed into the camo outfit I got, and grabbed one of Cade's shirts to pull over it. The shirt came down to my knees so it pretty much covered me.

After I fix my make-up and my hair, I wander down to the kitchen to make something for a late dinner.

At seven, Cade and Timber come in. Timber runs right to me, jumping up and down. "Hey, baby girl. I missed you." I pet the top of her head and proceed to pour some food in her bowl.

"Damn, I thought I would walk in and find you in something sexy." Cade laughs as he wraps me in a hug and gives me a sweet kiss. "Did you have fun?"

"More or less. Wait till you see what I got." I wink at him while dishing out the spaghetti I made.

"Can't wait," he whispers against my ear then slaps my butt. "I'll go wash up."

After I have dinner set up and Cade is washed, we sit down to eat. "So, what did you want to talk to me about?"

He swallows the bite he has then turns all serious on me. "I've been thinking about the ranch."

"Okay." I frown and wait for him to continue.

"I was thinking of an idea that would help the ranch get back on its feet better." He smiles and lets out a little laugh looking at his plate. "It's actually been a dream of mine for a few years now."

"Well, what is it. Spit it out, Masters." His smile is still in place when he looks up at me.

"I was thinking of starting a rodeo camp. Just in the summers. I'll understand if you..."

"I love it!" I bounce a little in my seat. "What made you think of this?"

He shrugs. "With all the traveling I did, I saw how so many kids weren't able to have the opportunity to learn to even ride a horse. So, I thought maybe we could start a camp and give that opportunity to kids."

Could he be any sweeter? "Oh, Cade." My food is forgotten. I get up, walk over, and crawl into his lap. "That's so sweet." I kiss him. Then I draw back. "But we don't have that type of money."

He sighs. "Don't be pissed."

I frown. "What's going on?"

"I won the championship last year..."

I wait for him to continue, but he doesn't. He just stares at me. "And?"

"I made a lot of money..."

"Okay. Please continue."

He runs a hand through his hair and sighs again. "I want to use part of the money to get the ranch out of the red. And then what is left, I want to use for equipment for a rodeo camp." He gets a crease in his forehead and waits for my reaction.

He won? I didn't know that because I didn't keep track of him. Dad possibly did, but I didn't. I bite my lip and nod. "Okay."

"Okay?" He looks happy and hopeful.

"Okay," I answer back with a smile. I bend down and give him another kiss against his smile.

He slides his hand up my bare thigh and freezes. I let out a little giggle. He found the garter belt to the outfit. He pulls back from our kiss and stares at me as a slow smile comes to his face. "Can I see now?"

I move off his lap and fix the shirt. "No, finish your dinner first, mister." I walk back over to my seat and go back to eating.

"Damn you, woman," he mutters then shovels his food down. *Silly man.*

After dinner, I decide to torment him. "Go shower. I'll do the dishes."

"Only if you join me." He wraps his arms around me and tries to pull his shirt over my head.

"Cade Nathan Masters." I bat his hands away. "Shower." I point to the door.

"You don't play fair," he pouts.

"I know. Now go." He frowns then makes his way up to the bedroom and to the bathroom. I quickly finish the dishes and make my way up to the bedroom. I pull his shirt over my head and try to find a sexy way to pose on the bed; this I am not good at.

Finally, I decide to lay on my side facing the bathroom. I feel my eyes grow heavy until I hear a sharp intake of air. I open them and see Cade standing there with one towel around his waist and another frozen halfway to his head. "Damn, baby." He grins dropping both towels and walks to me, growing excited.

Chapter Fourteen

TODAY IS FRIDAY, September 27th, Cade's birthday. I have everything ready to go, and I feel giddy. I have a nice dinner planned for us at the same steakhouse we went to on our first date. Then we are going to Hank's where everyone is waiting for us for a little surprise party, and then finally home where I plan on giving him his second birthday present.

I even bought myself a new dress for the occasion and had Libby curl my hair so I looked nice.

I managed to get all my chores done early today and boot scooted it to town to get ready at Libby and Maddi's. In the last month, they found a place for themselves. Libby was growing tired of having Clint come over to her mom's house.

Maddi's mood seems to have improved since our girls' day. I don't know much more than the fact that her and Tucker are talking to one another again, and my brother is finally trying to win her back.

Libby was pretty quiet while doing my hair. She didn't seem like her usual self which had me asking why. Not that I don't already know the answer; Clint.

"I just don't feel good, Em," she all but muttered to me as she put another curl in my hair.

"You getting sick or something?"

She shrugged. "I guess."

"Lib, talk to me." I looked up to see her head dropped low between her shoulders and then saw tears falling. "Oh, honey." I

My Cowboy

get up and wrap her in a hug. "What's going on?" *If he hurts her, I'll kill him.*

She buries her face in my shoulder. "I'm pregnant, Emma."

"W-what?" I'm shocked. If anything, Libby has always been safe. "You must not be that far along, Lib."

She shakes her head. "I found out last night," she says softly into my shoulder. "I have an appointment in a next week."

"And I'm now just finding out?" She nods. "Does Clint know?" She shakes her head no.

"No, I haven't told him yet. Only you and Maddi. I don't...I don't know how to tell him, Em." She shakes her head and sits down. "It was just supposed to be a fun fling. He just broke off his engagement with Stacy Poll two weeks before we started fucking around." Even sad, she's blunt. I'm glad this isn't shaking her too much.

"Wait ... when did you guys start?"

"Week before your graduation. Emma, what should I do?"

I straighten my shoulders out and look her right in the eyes. "You stand up tall like you always do. Tell him, and if he doesn't like it, fuck him. You are strong and don't need anyone. Well, except your mom, Maddi, and me." I smile at her, earning me a small one from her. "You can do this, Libby. Even if it means raising the baby on your own. You'll always have me." I hug her after she wipes her eyes.

"Thank you. You're right. I can do this." She smiles and stands. "Let's finish your hair." I nod and take the seat she just left. Never thought I would be the one to pull her back together.

~*~*~*~

I STILL CAN'T believe my best friend, my sister in all ways except blood, is pregnant. I'm still not sure where Maddi stands with Tucker, or should I say it the other way around. I'm lost in my thoughts waiting for Cade to finish cleaning up for dinner.

Cade clears his throat, pulling me from those thoughts. "Wow. Emma, you look stunning." I blush and take him in. He's in his usual get up; his amazing chest is cased in a dark blue button up, and new-ish Wranglers wrap around his muscular legs. Much like me, Cade doesn't have a good pair of jeans just for dress up, along with his boots, buckle, and hat. My sexy cowboy.

While I check him out, he does the same to me in return. I'm wearing a spaghetti strap navy blue sundress with my boots and a jean jacket. "Just stunning," he says as he takes me in his arms and kisses me sweetly.

"Happy Birthday," I quietly say, smiling up at him. "Ready for your birthday dinner?"

"You know it!" He grabs my hand and hauls me out the door to his truck.

On the way to dinner, I remain quiet by his side, still thinking about Libby and the Maddi-Tucker situation. Cade squeezes my knee, drawing my attention back to him. "What's wrong?"

I smile and shake my head. "Nothing." He gives me the look that he knows I'm lying. "I can't tell you yet. Not my secret to tell." I smile and give him a kiss. "Don't worry. Nothing bad."

He nods, taking my hand after he shifts.

"Sure you won't get food poisoning again?" Cade looks at me from across our little table.

"Not getting shrimp on the side this time. I think that's what did it." Nodding, he proceeds to tell the waiter what he would like then I do the same.

"I'm never going to get you to eat a medium rare steak, am I?"

"Nope. Not a chance. Even if you cook it and force it down my throat, I'll just spit it all over you," I tease as I slide my foot up his leg.

"Don't test me right now woman." He grinds his teeth together.

I lick my bottom lip. "Can I give you one of your presents right now?" His eyes get heated. "Not that type of present!" I throw my napkin at him. "I'm not Libby; I'm not an exhibitionist."

He gives me his panty-melting smile, destroying my panties. "Okay, what is it?"

I pull the little box out of my coat pocket and slide it toward him. "Figured you may have a use for this." Frowning and looking confused, he shakes it then starts to unwrap it. "Quit thinking naughty thoughts there, Masters. I wouldn't give you anything like that in a restaurant."

"A coyote call?" He smiles up at me.

"Figured you could use a good one instead of the piece of crap you've been using."

"Thank you, sugar." He gets up, walks over and gives me a kiss that no one in a restaurant should see. "That's a preview for later." He winks and returns to his seat. *Oh, boy.*

~*~*~*~

AS WE DRIVE down the road, I have yet to tell Cade to go to Hank's, but I probably should soon. He keeps sliding his hand up my bare leg. "Hey, head to Hank's. I think we should go dancing for a bit." I smile sweetly up at him.

"Ummm ... okay." He frowns more to himself and turns off the road to home, heading to Hank's instead.

Once we pull into the empty parking lot, Cade looks out toward the bar and sees there are no lights on. "I don't think he's open tonight."

"Really?" I look out. "Libby should be working." I get out of the truck. "Come on, let's go check it out." He nods as he climbs out his side.

We walk hand in hand up to the front door. I try it, and it's unlocked. "Well, it's unlocked. Come on." I pull him in behind me.

It's pitch black instead, but the second Cade walks in, the lights fly on and all our friends yell, "Happy Birthday," to him.

I turn around and smile up at him. "Surprise." He laughs and pulls me into his arms.

"Thank you." Kissing the top of my head, he then walks over to my brother, Justin, and Clint. I make my way to my mom and the girls.

~*~*~*~

AFTER A COUPLE of hours there, I've managed, with the help of Maddi, to cheer up Libby. She refuses, no matter what Clint says, to give up or get rid of the baby. Which makes me really happy.

"Dance with me, sugar." I look up over my shoulder and see Cade walking toward me. I turn back to Libby and smile.

"My cowboy wants to dance." I turn and skip into his arms. Man, since being with this guy, I've turned into such a girl!

Cade pulls me into the middle of the dance floor. It's only the two of us out there. The song is slow and low. Cade pulls me right up against him. His rough, hard body meets my small soft one. I could melt away in his arms.

"Thank you, Emma. This has been a great birthday."

I rub my cheek against his chest. "It's not over yet."

"What more could you do?"

I peek a look up at him. He's smiling down at me. His eyes are dancing with love. "I love you," I whisper. He stops moving and stares down at me in shock. *Shit!* I had this all planned out. *Damn son-of-a-bitch!* Have I misread all his facial expressions? Does he just see me as something fun? I start to pull away from him. I can't even bring myself to look him in the eye.

He doesn't let go and pulls me tight against him. Then he lifts me up to his lips. "I love you, too, Emma." He pulls me in for a kiss. *He loves me? He really does love me?* I return his kiss with my own. Knocking his hat off in the process of grabbing a hold of his hair and holding him tight against me.

"Get a room!" Clint yells from across the bar followed by him shouting, "Ow!" when Justin slugs him in the arm.

He pulls me back slightly. "Let's get out of here." I nod and giggle as he drags me toward the door. "Thank you, everyone!" he shouts as we make our way out.

~*~*~*~

I CAN BARELY manage to get the front door unlocked and opened with Cade assaulting my neck with kisses. "Cade," I whine.

I break free of him and step away from him. "Go sit in the living room. I still have one more present for you." He groans as I fly up the stairs to our room.

It takes me a while to change into the fantasy costume and gather my hair up to make it complete. I do a once-over in the mirror and nod at myself in approval.

I feel a little silly, but I know Cade will love it. Quietly, I make my way down to the living room. I sneak a peek around the corner and see him watching some TV while he waits for me. I nearly die when I see what he is watching. Go figure, the very movie my outfit comes from. I clear my throat. "Mind shutting that off."

"Umm ... yeah ... sure." Cade sits up and shuts it off. The only light in the room is coming from the lamp in the corner, making a soft glow through the whole area. I stand up straight and take a deep breath. *Here goes.*

I walk in with fake confidence. My eyes are cast downwards until I'm in front of him then I lift them. I can't help but laugh at Cade's expression. He was sitting back with one leg crossed over the other with one arm resting on the back of the couch. Now, he is sitting up straight, eyes wide, mouth hanging open.

I bite my lip and throw my head back. "Well, if you don't like it. I guess I'll ..." I start to walk away when he grabs me and pulls me onto his lap. The instant I touch his lap, I feel his hardened member under my butt.

"Damn, baby." He runs his fingers over the fabric of the skirt. "What made you think of this?" He looks up at me with glee and wonder.

"Well, you've always been a fan of Star Wars."

"Damn, I'm one lucky fucker." He grins and plays with my braid. "Thank you." He moves the chain collar on my neck and starts to kiss it, then lightly bites down. I moan.

He picks me up by my waist and moves me so I'm straddling him. I gently rock my hips into his causing him to moan. I move away to make quick work of his pants and underwear. He barks a quick laugh watching me fumble with his buckle. Damn thing is in the way.

Once I'm done, I move back to him. Kissing my way up his jaw to his ear that I lightly bite down on and pull, I whisper, "I don't have anything on under this."

With urgent speed, he moves his hand under the skirt and groans finding me bare underneath. He moves his fingers down to play with my clit then further down to my center where he pushes two fingers in. "Fuck...baby you're so wet."

I'm still kissing his neck and ear. "Only for the man I love." He hooks his fingers to my left side causing me to nearly jump off his lap. "And the only one to ever find my spot." I moan as I start to rock against his hand.

Since I was already worked up, it took me no time to climb and fall over the edge. "Cade!" I scream as I throw my head back and rock against him some more.

Once I've calmed down a bit, I look into his eyes. "I love you, sugar." He kisses me sweetly before sliding his tongue into my mouth.

My Cowboy

I grab a hold of him and pump him a few times causing his head to fall back. "I love you, too, cowboy." I roll some pre-cum around his head then bring him up to my opening and slowly push him into me. I hiss as he groans.

"Nothing feels better than you, Emma." He thrusts himself the rest of the way in, causing me to jump again.

I rock against him, but the damn skirt is pissing me off because it keeps sliding down and getting in my way. I make him laugh and groan at the same time by stopping and throwing the skirt over my shoulder. I place my hands on his shoulders and start to ride him.

"Yeah," he says as he kisses me then smacks my butt roughly causing me to go faster. He wraps his hands around my sides then moves up my back to undo my bra and release me. Once that is out of the way, he grabs a hold of me and starts to rub my nipples until they are hard and almost to the point of pain.

"Oh, Cade!" I roll my head back and keep going. When he pulls one of my nipples into his mouth and starts to suck and bite at it, I fall over the edge again. I slow my movements and grip onto him as tightly as I can, causing him to groan again but louder.

"Damn, Emma. It's so fucking hot watching you come." He thrusts up into me and starts to pound me.

Then he picks us up, not missing a beat, and lays me on the couch. He starts to thrust in and out harder and faster.

With one hand, he continues to play with my nipples while the other moves down, pressing circles around my clit. "Ooooo." I can't bring myself to form any words.

His moments became feral and crazed as my next climax crests, followed by his.

We still, both breathing uncontrollably. My heart feels like I just ran a marathon. I place my hand over his and feel that his heart is going just as fast. I look up into his eyes, and he smiles. "It's beating so fast for all the love I feel for you, Emma."

He leans down and gives me one last sweet kiss before he pulls out.

I go to stand but nearly fall over. "I can't feel my legs."

He laughs and picks me up. "Then I did a great job." He carries me up to our room. He makes me feel so cherished and loved with the way he takes care of me. He lays me on the bed, proceeding to the bathroom to get a washcloth to clean up and removes the costume. "I love the costume." He looks it over then puts it on the chest at the foot of the bed. He pulls one of his shirts over my head. "Thank you for an amazing birthday." He kisses each of my cheeks as we cuddle in bed together. "I love you, Emma Price."

I cuddle into his chest and smile. "I love you, too, Cade Masters."

Chapter Fifteen

I STEP OUT into the crisp early October morning. I love this time of year. Yesterday, Cade helped me find a deer, and now I'm heading down to cut him up for steaks, jerky meat, and ground meat. Then I'll be loading everything up to head up the mountain tomorrow and set up my camp before opening morning for elk hunting.

As I'm making my way down to the barn, my phone starts to go off. *Maddi.* "Hey chica, what's happenin'?"

"Morning, Em." She doesn't seem too cheery. That's the one thing about Maddi; she is always cheerful, even when life has her down.

"What's wrong?" I swing the barn door open and the boys look up at me. "Morning, lovelies," I say to them kissing both Stampede and Ripper on the nose then make my way to the back where my deer is hanging.

"Libby. I'm worried about her, Emma." *And here I thought it would be about Tucker. Thank God. They are finally figuring things out.*

"How? She seemed fine to me last night." I grab my knife and sharpening stone.

"Well, I'm not sure. She just seems off. Plus, I haven't seen Clint around here in a few days." With everything going on in her life, Maddi still puts others in front of her.

"Well, you know what I always say. Fuck 'em." I start in on the back straps. "Did she tell him? She hasn't said anything to me."

"Yes, they got into an argument. I really didn't hear what about, but he hasn't been back since. Emma, she may seem fine around everyone else, but once she is home, she isn't herself." She huffs at her end.

Shit, this isn't good. I feel bad. I've been so busy with things around the ranch I haven't been around much.

"Well, maybe after I get down, we can plan a girls' weekend of too much ice cream, bad romance movies, and fingernail painting to try and cheer her up."

"Sounds good to me. But over here. No boys allowed." I smile.

"No boys," I agree. "Well, in the meantime, can you do your best on your own? I'll try to come in this afternoon, but I'm leaving in the morning."

"Yeah, I can handle everything!" Now, that is the cheerful Maddi I know. "I got to go, I hear her getting up."

I laugh. "Okay. I'll be in later."

"Okay! Bye!"

"Bye." I slide my phone into my back pocket and get to work on the rest of my deer.

It only takes me about an hour to get him all cut up by myself. I skinned out his head and put it in my chest freezer so I could boil clean it when I get down the mountain for a European mount. I put his skin in a bag to take to town for the 'hides for vets' wagon to raise money for local veterinaries. Meat is all put away in the right freezers and my hands are washed. Time to load my truck.

~*~*~*~

I LOAD ONE of my saddles and all my camping gear into the horse trailer and check over the boys. I went inside to make a quick sandwich then decide to bring my bag down and put it in the truck. As I was throwing the last couple things into my bag, I hear a vehicle pull up out front.

I wasn't expecting anyone. My guess is that it is more than likely my mom. Cade, Tucker, Steven, and Timber are out pregchecking cows today and moving bulls into a separate pasture so I'm not expecting them back till later this evening. Timber has become Cade's little buddy. I suspect that he feeds her table scraps.

"Hello?" I hear a strange female voice and a knock on the screen door.

"Just a moment!" I yell down the stairs and zip my bag up. I fly down the stairs and see the back of a woman with long blond hair with dark brown roots. "May I help you."

The woman turns around and whoa! I come to a halt at the door and slowly open it. This woman is very heavily pregnant. "Hello." She smiles at me, but it doesn't reach her eyes.

"Can I help you?" I ask again. It's rude to not answer someone.

"Yes. Sorry." She glares slightly at me. "I'm looking for my fiancé."

I frown not understanding. "Okay, who's your fiancé?"

She rolls her eyes and rubs her huge belly. "Cade Masters. Is he here?"

What! I'm confused, Cade said he hasn't been with anyone in a few years. *Who the hell is this?* I blink a few times and shake my head. "And you are?"

"Chloe," she states. "Is he here or not?" Hello attitude, too bad you won't meet my fist. I will never lay a hand on a pregnant woman.

"No. He isn't." I cross my arms.

"Who are you?" Her attitude just gets more wonderful.

"Emma Price. And Cade hasn't said anything about you so I guess you can understand my shock."

"Oh, well tell him I've been trying to reach him and with the baby due soon, I need daddy there." Her smile pisses me off. I clench my fists then slowly let go. I need to keep myself in check.

"I'll be sure he gets the message."

"I could wait." She tries to walk past me.

"Umm ... I don't think so. This is my house. Maybe he could meet you wherever you're staying?" I give her my own evil smile.

"Fine. I'm at the Holiday Inn." She turns on her high heels and walks back to her car. No thank you, fuck you, suck my dick, nothing.

BITCH! Don't let my calm demeanor with her fool you. I'm pissed, beyond pissed! *That fucker Masters lied to me! Only you, Emma, bullshit.*

I've been cheated on and I would never want to be the other woman. I know how it feels. And he has a fucking fiancée pregnant with his kid. He said he couldn't have any, obviously that was a lie, too.

The taste of blood makes me realize I am biting down on my tongue. I look down at my bag and make my decision. "Fuck this shit!" I slam the doors shut and take off toward my truck.

I load Stampede first because he is always easier to load. Ripper always takes some time and once he sees his brother in the trailer, he usually follows him in. I don't know what the deal is with him lately, but he's been jumpy.

I peel out of headquarters and head for the mountains. I call my mom.

"Hey, Mom."

"Hi, sweetie. How is everything?" She sounds winded.

"Did I catch you at a bad time, Mom?"

"No ... just ran in from the garden when I heard the phone ring. Is everything okay, sweetie? You sound irritated."

"No, just wanting to let you know I'm heading up the mountain today instead."

"Oh. Getting the itch pretty bad?" She laughs.

"Yep. That's it, Mom. Well, I wanted to let you know. I'll be up Kearny Pass until I get something."

"Okay, sweetie, be safe. I love you."

My Cowboy

"Love you, too, Mom."

"Bye."

"Bye." I hit the end button and tap on the steering wheel. I better call Libby to let her know what just happened. I don't want Mom knowing because then she will tell Tucker, and I'm not ready for that showdown yet.

"Hey!" She sounds like herself.

"Hey, Lib." This phone call I don't try to hide my anger.

"Ah oh, what happened?"

"He has a fucking fiancée, Lib, and a baby!"

"What! Who?"

"Cade fucking Masters." I take a deep breath. "I was packing the truck up when this bottle-blond shows up and basically demands to know where Cade is. She's pregnant, heavily." I feel like breaking down, but I won't. I haven't cried in ten years, and I'm not about to start.

"Oh, Emma."

"Don't worry. I just wanted to let you know. Don't tell anyone, okay?"

She sighs. "Do you always have to be this way?"

"What do you mean?"

"Breakdown, get pissed, break something, for fuck's sakes. Don't bottle it up."

"Hunting will help. All the time I need to focus on finding an elk will help. I'll be up Kearny Pass."

"Okay." She drags out. "Be safe, please."

"I always am."

"Bye, chica. See you in a few days."

"Bye. Take care of you and baby. Love ya."

"Lova ya, too."

~*~*~*~

I IGNORE MY phone, which rings about half a dozen times on the way up the face of the mountain, until I lose cell service.

I pull into the parking area that is the head of many different trails around the Kearny Pass area. As I am unloading the boys and getting them all ready to go, another vehicle pulls up.

"Well, hello there, Emma."

I looked over Stampede's back to see my old high school history teacher getting gear out of his truck. "Hello, Mr. Reed." I smile. "Going hunting?"

"Yes, I am. Ready to find the big one this year." He smiles at me. "I see you have the same plans."

"I do." I check to see if everything is down tight on Stampede before mounting Ripper. "Good luck with your hunt, Mr. Reed."

"And you, Emma. Find the big one." He waves at me as I start to move the boys up the trail.

~*~*~*~

ABOUT FIFTEEN MINUTES later, the boys and I are making pretty good timing heading up to my usual campsite when Ripper starts acting skittish. My stomach has been in knots since we left the house earlier, but I'm sure it has to do with the bastard known as Cade Masters.

"Really, Ripper? What is up with you?" I try to urge him to keep going but he is being stubborn and walking backward.

"Ripper!" I kick him in the sides, but it does me no good. Then I feel a pull on my leg and look over at Stampede who is doing the same as his brother. "What is going on, you two!?!"

I try to get them both going forward again, but neither are behaving. "Fuck!" Just as I move forward in my saddle, Ripper's head comes back, hitting me right in the face.

The next thing I know, there is an intense sharp pain in my right side and Ripper falls to our left pinning my leg under his side.

"Shit!" Ripper quickly moves to get up, dragging me a little before my foot falls out of the stirrup. Something heavy comes down on me, and the last thing I see is Ripper running back down the trail through a grove of aspens, where we just came from, his side covered in blood.

"No ... Rip ... per." I reach out for him doing me no good.

Then there is nothing. No light, just pain. The last thing I remember before everything goes black is the sound of Stampede baying like a horse trying to be broke.

Then.
There.
Was.
Only.
Darkness.

Chapter Sixteen

IN MY LIFE, I tried to be the very best person my momma raised me to be. When Gema's heart started to give when I was pulling Stampede and Ripper out, I swore to her that I would be the very best mom to her boys as I possibly could be.

When Dad and I found a half frozen Roundhouse clinging to his dead mother, I again swore to raise him and be a mom to him.

I always thought of myself as a good person, even if I never boasted about it. Through everything I've been through, the loss of my dad especially, I've remained a strong person, never giving up to take an easier road.

I worked hard for everything I have and everything I ever wanted. Hell, I broke my first horse at the age of seven. Rode a bull at ten and became the owner of Price Cattle Company and Ranch at the age of twenty-four. I'm proud of myself.

I survived many things and I will survive whatever the hell has me down now, even if it means I wake up with a broken heart.

~*~*~*~

AFTER SO MUCH darkness, I was finally able to open my eyes, just to close them again. The blinding white almost did my eyes in. Slowly, I ease my eyes open to the absolute white that now surrounds me.

Where am I? As I get everything into focus, I see that I am in a field of winter wheat, but it's different shades of light gray and white kind of like the old movies. The sky above me is white, the trees and the hillsides are as well.

My Cowboy

I look down and see I am also in a white sundress, kind of like the one I own. My boots are even white! My hair falls in waves, framing my face in curls.

I look up with a frown and look around me. I'm all alone. But then I feel a strange pull and urge to turn around. When I do, I see a figure in the distance. It's too far away to know for sure whether it is coming or going.

So, I start moving toward it but stop soon when I come to a little brook. I stand there and watch the figure as it gets closer and closer.

It's a man on a horse. They are both white and the man's head is hung down with his hat covering his face. As they draw closer, I suck in a breath of air. I recognize the horse first. "Gema," I whisper, drawing my fisted hand to my heart. *My beautiful Gema, what is she doing...here?*

When the rider stops Gema right on the other side of the brook from me, he dismounts and finally looks up at me. "Dad?" He gives me a weak lopsided smile before it turns into a frown. "Daddy!" I jump across the brook right into his warm embrace.

I'm dead...I have to be.

"You ain't supposed to be here yet, princess." I draw back and look up at my dad questioning him with my eyes. "Come on, let's take a walk." He grabs my hand as I look back at Gema. "Don't worry, she'll follow; she's waitin' for someone."

"Okay," I whisper. *Why am I in a field with my dad?*

"Because this is where the good Lord sent you." My dad smiles down at me then looks down to my right side and frowns once more.

"You can hear my thoughts?"

"I'm one of your angels, princess. I can hear everything." He brings my hand up and kisses it. "I've missed you."

"I've missed you, too, Dad."

"You're doing a good job, Emma. I'm very proud of you."

I simply nod, trying to control my emotions. "Here he comes now." My dad points up, I follow seeing a figure coming toward us.

"Nate?"

My dad laughs. "No, Nate is back where I came from watching Cade. Let me tell you; he was pissed about what Cade pulled after his death." He turns me in his arms into another hug. "He's glad Cade is back where he belongs." Dad hugs me tightly. "Where he always belonged."

I don't answer. I still feel hurt from what Cade lied about. "Let him explain, princess." He pulls me back and looks down into my eyes. "Okay?" I simply nod.

"Jackson?"

"Nope." He shakes his head. "Again, he's back with Nate watching over Libby and her baby." He gets a weak smile. "She'll be a good momma."

"She will be."

"Thank you for having faith in your brother, Em. He needs all of you."

"He needed you, too." I look up at him.

"I'm always with him now, just like I am with you." He looks out into the distance. "He and Maddi will be okay."

My head shoots up when I hear the sound of hooves beating against the ground. I look up where the figure was and see Stampede running toward us.

"No...no! Not my boy!" I jerk out of my dad's arms and run to my baby boy. He comes to a stop in front of me as I run to him. He brings his face down to mine as the tears fall. "No!" I try my best to wrap my arms around his neck and bury my face in his neck as I cry uncontrollably.

I feel my dad's strong weathered hands grab my bare shoulders. "Let it out, Emma. It's okay to cry, princess."

My Cowboy

I turn and bury myself in my dad's chest once again trying to get my tears under control. "Just let it happen." He rubs my back.

"Wh...wh...what happened, Daddy?" I look up at him through the tears in my eyes.

Gently, he wipes the tears away. "You were attacked by a mountain lion." He looks at Stampede and rubs his hand over some marks on his back that were never there before. "He saved you, Emma. He saved the one person he always had as a mother. These are the scars he will carry for eternity up here, and he'll wear them with pride." He smiles down at me then frowns once again at my right side. "Some people up here carry their scars on the outside like Stampede, Nate, and Jackson while others carry them on the inside like I do." He puts both of our hands over his heart.

"What about me, Dad?"

He shakes his head. "You aren't supposed to be here, Emma." He pulls me back to arm's length. "Your mother and brother need you. Maddi needs you. Libby really needs you and so does Cade, Emma." I go to speak, but he silences me much like he did when he was alive. "But you need them, too. I'm so very proud of you, princess, but you carry too much on your own. You fight from letting anyone in." He smiles and shakes his head more than likely thinking of a good example. "You carry so much. Don't be afraid to ask for help and admit that you are weak in some points. I know you too well. Let yourself cry, allow yourself to need help on something for me, please."

I nod up at him trying to smile, but it doesn't come.

"I wish I could still be there with you." I look up to the tears now in his eyes. Frank Hunter Price never cried. "To walk you down the aisle at your wedding, to hug you and hold my grandchildren and to just hold all of you again." I wipe his tears. "Just remember I'll always be up here making sure you are all okay. And right here," he points to my head, "where I taught you life lessons that I expect my grandchildren to learn as well. And here," he points to my heart, "where all the love I gave you will remain forever and always."

I start to cry again and hug him once more.

I feel him move his fingers to my shoulder blades. "I love that you got this to remember me by." He kisses my forehead. "But Emma, it's time for you to go." He taps on the halo at the base of my neck. "I love you so much, Emma. I promise to watch over you till we can be here together again."

"I love you, too, Daddy."

Then everything goes dark again Gema nestled up with Stampede, and my dad smiling down at me. I'm alone once more.

Chapter Seventeen

"PLEASE, DEAR LORD, don't take her from me." My mom's broken voice comes to my ears. "Please don't take my baby girl. I need her so much. Please." I feel some pressure on my left side and a cold hand grab mine. "Oh, Emma, wake up. Let me see your beautiful blue eyes again. Mommy needs you, sweetie." I feel her head fall on my shoulder lightly. "Please don't leave me." She starts crying.

"Mmmm."

"EMMA!" I feel her jump a little.

"Mmm..ooo..mmm?" I slowly try to open my eyes, but it hurts.

"OH! Thank God!" she cries.

After a couple of tries, I manage to open my eyes. There is faded light everywhere. I look around and see my brother in a darkened corner, arms crossed. I look toward my mom. It hurts to keep my eyes open.

"Hi, Mom." I try to offer her a smile, but it hurts too much.

"Hi, sweetie." Gently, she brushes her hand through my hair. "I missed you."

"Missed you, too." My throat felts really dry. "Ripper..."

"He's fine sweetie, Mr. Reed got him under control and to the vet."

I smile then close my eyes and darkness takes me again.

~*~*~*~

"PLEASE, BABY COME back to me. I don't know what to do without you." Cade's voice brings me out of the darkness. "I love you so much, Emma. I was messed up for so long and now that we are finally together, I feel that I can actually live." He grabs my left hand. "That I have a reason to live." I feel his lips on my hand.

I moan and roll my head. Slowly, I open my eyes. It still hurts but not as bad. The first thing I see are the blinds drawn in the window, but I can still tell it is dark out.

"Fuck." I manage to lift my right hand to my head.

"Oh, baby. Thank God." Cade comes up and kisses my forehead.

"Baby, my ass, you dipshit!" The best I can, I push him away from me.

"What ... Emma?" He looks shocked and confused.

I look around and find a tissue box next to my bed. I pick it up and throw it at him. "Get the fuck out of here!" I yell as he backs up toward the door.

"Emma!" He manages to dodge the box. Then I find a ball of yarn sitting there, and I throw it at him, too.

"Go find your fucking fiancée and get the hell out of my fucking life!" I yell louder this time.

"What the fuck is going on with you, Emma!" he yells back and dodges the ball of yarn as well.

"You fucking lied to me, you jackass!" The next thing I know, I have my mom's knitting needles in my hand ready to throw at him but don't get the chance because my room door swings open hitting Cade square in the face.

A pissed off nurse marches in. Cade shuts the door rubbing his face and glaring at me. "Will you two stop." She places her hands on her hips. I hear another door open and shoot a look at my mom coming out of my bathroom, but she stops. "She doesn't need this stress on herself or the baby."

"Baby!" Cade and I both yell at the same time.

The nurse nods. "Calm down. I'm going to go call the doctors to let them know you are awake." She turns and leaves.

My Cowboy

"I'm not pregnant!" I point at Cade. "His fucking buckle bunny fiancée is the pregnant one!" I look at Cade who slowly moves to the small chair next to my bed and drops his massive body into it, mumbling it's not possible. He looks ashen and dazed.

I turn to my mom. "What is going on, Mom?" I somehow manage to cross my arms minus all the IVs in my hands.

She is still standing at the bathroom door with tears in her eyes and one hand over her heart. "It's a miracle." She moves to me quickly.

"I can't be, Mom." I shake my head in disbelief. "Even if I was, I was thrown from Ripper..." I trail off as she shakes her head no.

"When they brought you in that Friday, they ran all sorts of tests and a pregnancy test was one of them. It came back positive, sweetie." She bends down and kisses my forehead. "Only I knew and I kept it to myself till just now." She grabs one of my hands and places it on my belly with hers. "Our little miracle," she whispers.

"I'm so confused." I throw my head back on my pillow, but it hurts. "Ow!"

~*~*~*~

TEN MINUTES OF talking it over with my mom and the nurse, who were both telling me that I was indeed pregnant, four glasses of water, and still no movement from Cade, the doctor walks in.

"Glad to see you awake young, lady." He shakes my hand. "I'm Dr. Mason."

"Nice to meet you," I mumble. I'm still in shock. Libby is the pregnant one, not me.

"Well, let's take a look at you." He has me sit up and goes about checking my eyes, head, shoulders, and arms. "Well, you don't have a concussion, but you'll still be sporting two black eyes for a while." I nod.

"Why does my left leg hurt so much?" I groan. "I remember Ripper landing on it and dragging me a few feet but ..."

"You have a pretty bad sprain. You're lucky it didn't break." Dr. Mason pulls the covers off my left leg and starts to check it over. "When you're ready, we will have the physical therapist come in and help you with walking."

I nod. "Okay. I'm ready." I try to get up but hiss at the pain in my right side.

He laughs and shakes his head. "Oh, no, you're not, young lady." It seems my hiss snapped Cade out of his daze, and he is on the left side of my bed with my mom in a flash. "Now, if you can, roll to your left side so I can take a look at your scratches."

"Scratches?"

"Yes." Dr. Mason goes about lifting my shirt while Cade and my mom help me balance on my left side. He slowly takes the bandages off.

"Shit!" Once they are off, I look down at four scratches that start at the bottom of my ribcage and wrap around my side to the top of back of my hip bone. "No wonder Dad kept frowning at my side," I mutter, making everyone look at me, confused.

"They aren't deep, but you will have to take special care of them." He starts to clean them. I look away quickly because it hurts. "We'll teach you how to care for them but for now myself and the nurses will do it." I just nod and keep my eyes close.

Once he's done, he puts clean bandages over them and helps me roll onto my back. "You are very lucky, young lady." He pats my right leg before leaving. "I'll be back to check on you later. I'm going to go talk to the physical therapist. Take care of yourself."

I nod as he leaves. I look back at my mom and glare at Cade. "I'm going to go make calls to let everyone know you are awake and doing okay," my mom says as she heads out the door as well.

My Cowboy

"'Kay, Momma." I smile at her as she shuts the door. Then I turn a death glare at Cade. "You better start talking, Masters."

For the first time since I've woken up, I notice how he looks. His hair is a mess, he hasn't shaved, and it looks like he hasn't changed his clothes in a while.

"Jesus, baby." He slowly sits on the right side of my bed taking my hand. I try to pull it from him, but he won't let go. "First of all, I'm glad to see you again. You had us worried."

I frown. "How long have I been out? I remember waking up to Mom and Tucker for a few seconds."

He nods. "That was Tuesday. It's early Saturday morning now."

"I've been out for a week!"

He shakes his head. "No. Two weeks."

I rub my left hand over my face, but do it too hard making it hurt. "Who's Chloe, Cade?" I scowl at him once again. "And no changing the subject."

He frowns. "How do you know about her?" he says with an almost disgusted voice.

"She showed up at the house, very pregnant, demanding to see her fiancé ... you!" I growl.

He stands and runs his hands through his hair. "And you believe her?"

I nod and glare up at him. "Why shouldn't I? You barely ever talk about the last ten years. You showed up out of nowhere."

"Emma." He comes back down to my side, grabs my hand in both of his, and pulls them to his chest. "I haven't been with Chloe in two years." He shrugs. "I left her after she slept with one of my buddies. And I didn't even ever sleep with her." He kisses my hand. "We were together briefly. You're the first in a long time." He looks me right in the eyes. "Feel that? You're the only one to make my heart beat like this."

I draw back a bit and still maintain my frown. "I never lied to you, baby. You brought me back to life. I love you so much." He brings his hand down to my belly. "I'll love you both for the rest of my life."

I'm about to speak when there is a light knock at the door then my OB/GYN Dr. Jen walks in.

Cade moves away back to my left side. "Now can you please explain to me how you didn't know you were pregnant?" Dr. Jen places her hands on her hips. One of the things I love about her is that she just says what's on her mind. No bullshit.

I shrug. "Been too busy to know?" I grimace. She shakes her head and turns as the same nurse who first came in walks in with an ultrasound machine.

"Thank you, Hannah." Hannah nods then leaves again. Dr. Jen turns back to me. "Remember your last period?" I shake my head no. It's true; I've been really busy. She sighs, rolls her eyes, and brings the machine over to me. "Well, let's check baby out, shall we?" She looks up at Cade. "Daddy?" He just nods

She plugs the machine in and goes about inputting my information. Thank God they already took the catheter out. She gets the wand ready and turns to me. "Can you at least prop your right leg up for me. Just like with your examines?" I nod.

"Whoa! Wait, you're not putting that ET finger in her, are you?" Cade's eyes are huge.

"Yes, I need to see how far she is, and I'm guessing not that far. In which case, a vaginal ultrasound needs to be done because the baby will still be pretty low down and very small." She laughs and looks back at me. "Ready?" I nod.

"Damn!" I jump a little, sending Cade into a frenzy. I grab his hand "Stop, it's just cold." He nods, and we both turn to the screen.

"Well, let's see if we can find baby." Dr. Jen moves the wand around until she stops. "There baby is." She points to the screen. "Little guy or gal is trying to hide." She moves the wand again and the baby comes up on the screen a little better.

"Oh, my ..." I choke on my words.

"So little," Cade whispers.

Dr. Jen nods. "Yep, let's get some measurements real quick then we will listen to the heart." We both nod and watch her work. She goes about typing things. "Well let's see...baby is measuring around seven to seven and a half weeks." She smiles down at me. She then stops typing and zooms in more and points to the screen. "See that part moving?" I nod while Cade whispers yes. "That's the baby's heart-beat, and it looks good. Want to hear?"

"Of course."

She turns up the volume, and we hear a small steady heartbeat coming through the speakers. "It sounds so fast," Cade says in wonder. I start to cry. My baby, my sweet little baby I had no clue about, is okay inside me after everything.

"Yep, baby heart rates are always fast. Sounds wonderful." She smiles at us. "You're very lucky, Emma." She starts pushing buttons and typing again. "I'll print some pictures."

Our eyes are glued to the screen as she does her work and looks over the baby, our baby. Even though it doesn't look like one yet, I love him or her with all my heart. "Everything looks amazing." She smiles once more at me then pulls the wand out.

Cade helps me put my gown back in order while Dr. Jen cuts the pictures up for us then hands them over. She does some paperwork. "I'll set up the appointments and call you with them." I nod. "Your due date looks to be right around June thirteenth, okay?" Again I nod.

"Speechless, hmm?" She nods. "Tends to happen with surprises. Congratulations, you two." She looks up at Cade with a serious look. "Take good care of her."

"I plan on it." He shakes her hand, and she gets the ultrasound machine ready to leave. Cade pulls out his wallet and puts one of the ultrasound pictures in it then hands me the rest.

"I'll come check on you a couple more times before you leave. Feel free to call me whenever you need."

~*~*~*~

HALF AN HOUR later we are still sitting on my bed looking over the pictures. "I can't believe you're carrying my son."

"Son?" I look up at Cade, who smiles and nods.

"Yep. Strong boy just like his daddy." He grins with pride while flexing his arms. "I love you, Emma. I promise to always take care of you two." He leans over and kisses my forehead.

"I love you, too," I whisper.

"Don't worry about Chloe. She'll go away." He wraps me in a hug carefully and kisses me again. "We'll get married, and she'll leave."

I start laughing even though it hurts. "Whoa there, cowboy. I'm not marrying you just because we are having a baby together." His face falls. "Besides, that was a shit of a proposal. Do better next time."

He shakes his head but smiles at me. Then gets up to go refill my water.

The room door flies open and Tucker storms in with a limp and a death glare on Cade. "You fucking bastard!"

Chapter Eighteen

TUCKER DRAWS BACK and decks Cade right in the side of his face.

"Tucker, stop!"

"You think you can just sweet talk your way to my sister! You've always been a brother to me, and I was finally getting used to the idea of you dating my sister!" Tucker hits him again.

Why the hell isn't Cade trying to stop him? I sit up a little too fast, causing all the air to leave me. Cade looks up at me and quickly moves away from my brother to my side.

"Tucker ..." I try to catch my breath. "Back off!" I shoot a glare at him.

Hannah comes running in, looking at the three of us. She shakes her head and walks back out muttering something about too much drama for one room.

"What the hell, Emma?" Tucker storms over to the opposite side of my bed from Cade. "You know about his fiancée and that she's pregnant, right?" He points at Cade.

I'm still trying to catch my breath while Cade eased me back down. "I don't have a fiancée, Tucker," Cade growls. "And getting Emma hyped up and stressed isn't good for her or *our* baby." After he gets me settled in, he pulls the ultrasound picture from his wallet and thrusts it in Tucker's face.

Tucker is still glaring at Cade when he grabs the picture then his expression changes as his eyes soften looking over the picture.

He looks at me then back at the picture then to Cade. "You're having a baby?" I nod.

"Are you calm now?" Cade folds his muscular arms over his amazing chest glowering at my brother.

Tucker simply nods and smiles at me.

I smile back and rub my belly on instinct. "How do you know about Chloe, Tucker?" I ask him.

Tucker shakes out of it and looks from Cade back to me while handing Cade his picture back. "I was in grovelling at Maddi's feet at the diner when this pregnant lady comes walking in asking for help to find her fiancé. So, being the nice guy I am..." I roll my eyes to that, "...I ask who her fiancée is, and she said you and that she was having your baby soon." Tucker's fists tighten then relax just thinking about it. "Then I got here as fast as I could to get you away from my sister."

Cade pinches the bridge of his nose between his eyes and shakes his head. "Fuck," he mutters. I grab his hand and when he looks down at me, he smiles. "I'm going to get you more water and ice."

"Okay," I whisper. He kisses my forehead and walks out the door. I turn my attention to my big brother. "Groveling?" I shoot an eyebrow up at him the best I can. *My face is killing me.*

Tucker pulls up a chair next to me. "God, I'm glad you're okay. You had us all worried."

"Thank you. I'm glad I'm fine, too, but don't change the subject."

He lays his head on the side of my bed and exhales, loudly. "I came to realize how badly I fucked up with Maddi.

My Cowboy

Seeing how broken you looked and how much everyone, including me, was hurting…I just couldn't be without her anymore." He shakes his head. "I fucked up."

"That you did," I state.

"Thanks for the sympathy, sis," he says dryly to me.

"You're welcome." It's his turn to raise a brow at me. "What? It's the truth and now you get to try and win her back, which is going to be extremely hard." I cross my arms. "She loves you so much, Tucker, but you hurt her big time by sleeping with someone else. Take it like a man and try your best to work it out. I want her as a sister." I stick my tongue out at him earning a sigh and a head shake.

"You're right."

"Of course, I'm right. I always…" He scowls down at me. "Usually right." I give him a quick smile.

"Right." He pats his legs. "I'm off." He bends down and kisses my forehead. "Love ya, sis."

As he makes his way to the door, it opens and in walks Cade, who looks really annoyed and Libby following him chewing his ass.

"And I mean it! I'll castrate you and not just chopping off your dick, I mean a hot rod shoved up your pee hole!"

I can't contain my laughter, but it hurts. Cade is this big guy being threatened by a little pistol like Libby. *This is great.* He brings my water to me and shakes his head. Then turns to sit down.

"You listening to me, Masters? Get the hell out!" She puts her hands on her hips and glares at him. She then looks at Tucker and me and we start laughing, even though I stop too soon. This sucks. "What?"

"Lib, it's okay." I nod. "We talked it out, and I know the truth. No fiancée, no baby...well at least her baby isn't his."

"What?" She looks confused.

Cade and Tucker move to the door. "I'll let you two talk, sugar. I'm going to run home and get some things for us." I nod and blow him a kiss as they head out.

"What the fuck?" She sits down at the end of my bed.

I take a deep breath. This is going to be hard work.

~*~*~*~

"WOW."

"That's all you have to say. Wow?" I frown at her.

"Well, what do you want me to say?" She shrugs. "That bitch. Wait till I find her."

"Feisty and pregnant. So sexy, Lib." I wink at her.

She huffs. "All in all, I'm glad that you're okay." She grimaces. "Even though I can't wait till you look like my best bitch again."

"Thanks."

"Seriously, two black eyes? Not a good look on you." She moves on my bed. "I'm really glad you're with us."

"Dad said you all needed me." I smile at her.

"Your dad?" She shakes her head. "I don't think I want to know. I've been pretty emotional lately. I really don't feel like crying."

"Well, I have some news for you that may make you cry." I play with my sheets and smile at her.

"What?" She's excited but trying to play it off.

"Don't freak, okay? I don't need my nurse coming in here again." She nods. "Okay. Here it goes." I take a deep breath.

"Out with it, Price!" she shouts.

My Cowboy

I glare at her and wait a second for my door to fly open once more. When it doesn't, I look back at her. "I'm pregnant."

She's frozen with a smile on her face then shakes her head. "No, you're not. I am. Did you forget that?" I roll my eyes. "Cade can't have kids; that's what you told me."

I look away. "Well...I am." I look back at her.

"Seriously?"

I nod.

"Oh. My. GOD!" She jumps up and down in her seat.

"Calm down," I groan and lay my head back closing my eyes.

When I look back up at her, I see tears in her eyes. "Seriously? We are going to have babies together?" She starts to blubber. "They'll be best friends just like us and our moms."

I smile at her and open my arms to bring her into a hug. She really starts crying, and I pat her on the head.

She pulls back and fans her face. "I'm so excited."

"Really? I couldn't tell?" I smile at her.

"If you weren't so hurt, I'd slap you."

"Love you, too."

She gets up off the bed, runs to the bathroom for a tissue, and comes back wiping her eyes. "I really am excited. I don't have to go through all of this by myself now. But oh! Wait! You'll be too big to be in the delivery room with me. But I really need you there." I go to speak but she continues. "Oh, well! We'll figure it out!" She smiles at me, and I smile back.

My door opens once more revealing my mom and Maddi. Maddi quietly walks up to me with tears in her eyes and wraps me in a hug without a word. I feel my shoulder grow wet. "It's okay, Mad."

She cries for a few more minutes just holding onto me. "Don't ever do anything like that to us ever again!" she quietly shouts into my shoulder. I nod my head and hug her tighter.

"I promise."

I look up to see my mom and Libby both crying. *Really?* "Were you all really that scared?"

"Of course, we were, Emma Jo!" My mom admonishes me.

Maddi pulls away nodding like Libby and steps back. "You're the glue."

"I'm the glue?" I'm confused.

"You keep us all together." Libby smiles.

I nod. "I'm needed." Smiling weakly, I start to cry. "I am really needed now." I nod.

The four of us sit and cry for a few minutes until the door opens and Dr. Mason walks in with Hannah and Cade.

Cade looks at all of us confused but then rushes to me when he sees I'm crying. "I'm fine," I whisper to him, and I melt into his arms.

"How are you feeling this evening, Emma?" Dr. Mason asks as he makes his way through my mom and the girls to me.

"I'm feeling all right. Still in some pain but overall," I nod, "good."

"That's great. Let me take a look at you then dinnertime and bed. You need rest."

I laugh. "Even though I've been out for two weeks?" He nods and smiles. "Ummm." I look up at Cade.

"What, sugar?"

I look back at Dr. Mason. "Before you begin, I need to use the restroom."

Dr. Mason nods and turns to Hannah. "Hannah, could you go get Emma a wheelchair please."

"Of course."

"Not necessary." Cade gently picks me up and starts to carry me to the bathroom. Since I no longer have as many IVs and the monitors are gone, I'm free to move around the best I can.

"Cade!" I quickly wrap my arms around his neck. "You are not putting me on the toilet!" I glare right into his beautiful browns.

He gives me half a grin. "I'll do whatever I need to for you, baby." He kisses me chastely then plops me down on the toilet. "Do your business."

Looking startled, I blush. Yes, I can blush, then I scold at him. "Leave. The. Room," I growl at him. He gives me his panty-melting grin, laughs, and walks out.

Before I go about my business, as Cade refers to it, I hear him getting chewed out by my mom and Dr. Mason. While Libby cheers him on.

Once I'm done, I try to stand to wash my hands, but it really hurts to put any pressure on my left foot. "Fuck," I mutter. Well, Mr. Masters must have been listening because the door opens and I'm in his arms once again. Not that I mind. *Nope, not one bit.*

He starts to take me back to my bed. "I need to wash my hands, mister muscles." Turning me back around, I wash up then back to bed for me.

"Now, Emma, let's have a look-see." Nodding, I take a deep breath readying myself to look at my scratches again.

Chapter Nineteen

THE NEXT MORNING, I am able to eat a lot more and change my clothes with Cade's help. I am just finishing my juice when there is a knock at the door. Dr. Jen and Dr. Mason have both already been in to check me over, so I'm not sure who it is.

When Cade opens the door, in walks a little round bubbly woman. "Morning. I'm Betty. I'll be helping you with your physical therapy, Emma." She smiles brightly at me.

It's too early for a good mood like this. I groan and lie back down. Taking a deep breath, I come back up. "Okay, let's get going on this."

"That's the spirit." She claps then looks up aa Cade. "My, you're a big boy." He just smiles. *No idea how big of a boy he is, lady.* I shake my dirty thoughts gone. "Well, you can help us by steadying her." Cade's smile gets bigger.

"Anything to get my hands on my beautiful girl." He winks at me.

I roll my eyes as I move my legs over the side of the bed.

~*~*~*~

THREE DAYS LATER and I'm walking steady again. The swelling around my eyes has gone down and my scratches are starting to itch.

Cade brought me some of my sweats and a few of his shirts. Must be a guy thing, marking me or something with his scent. Honestly, I wouldn't mind if he just peed on me if I could wear my own damn shirts again!

Libby and I are currently walking down one of the hallways in the hospital. Cade is never far behind me. He says it's just in case I fall or something. His grandma visited yesterday and was extremely excited to hear the baby news. Which! Cade still thinks baby is a boy. Me? I don't care as long as he or she is healthy, happy, has a good strong heartbeat, and ten fingers and ten toes.

Our walk has led us to the nursery. Libby and I stop and look down at the few babies that are currently in there. "I can't wait." Libby rubs her hand over her tiny baby bump.

"Me, either." I smile up at Cade, who bends down and kisses me on the forehead.

"There you are! Where in the hell have you been?" I stand perfectly still. *Yeah right, like that will make me invisible.* Cade's lips are frozen to my forehead. "I just had your son yesterday. Ready to see him?"

All three of us turn to see Chloe standing there expectantly. "Well?" She looks up at Cade. Then marches forward trying to grab him and drag him off.

"He isn't mine," Cade's voice booms making Chloe freeze and my panties melt. Love it when my cowboy gets this way.

"What do you mean, he isn't yours?" She can't even look him in the eyes. She pushes past me, nearly knocking me over to get to the nursery window. "There." She points down to a little blue bundle. She looks back at Cade. "That's Wyatt, your son."

Cade steadies me. "Go look," I whisper. "We'll head back to my room." I grab Libby and start to move away.

"No." Cade grabs my hand. "Together. We both know he isn't mine." I nod. Following Cade, we look down at the sleeping baby boy. *Oh, my God!*

"Oh, my God!" Libby reads my thoughts. "He looks nothing like him, you stupid cunt!"

Chloe stares shocked at Libby while Cade and I let out a little laugh. I look at the baby. He has really light features like Chloe if she were orange from tanning so much. He has no hair and one thing is for sure, Cade is a hairy guy; he's always had a full head of hair, even in his baby pictures.

There is no Cade in the baby; whoever his dad is, I feel sorry for both of them.

"Get lost, Chloe." Cade turns us, and we leave the maternity wing to go back to my room.

"You haven't heard the last of me, Cade," Chloe's annoying voice speaks up. "He is your son, and I'll prove it."

I stand up a bit straighter, the best I can do with my scratches. I turn around and get up in her face. Though she towers over me, I manage to get her to cower to me. "Back. The. Fuck. Off," I growl at her making her step back. "The only reason you think you can do anything to get him is because you know he won that money last year and it took you forever to track him down, right?" She's in shock. "Baby Daddy not want anything to do with you?" She still hasn't said anything; her mouth is hanging wide open. "Leave and I mean it." I turn around, grab Cade's and Libby's hands, but stop and look over my shoulder. "Oh, and, by the way, you look like hammered hog shit." With that, I march off the best I can.

~*~*~*~

GIVEN A CLEAN bill of health, I was finally sent home after another week in the hospital and physical therapy, but the bedrest I was ordered to was driving me absolutely crazy halfway through the first day. Prison guard Cade wouldn't let up. Even if he had work to do around the ranch, he would have my mom, Libby, or Maddi come *hang out* with me. *More like babysit me!*

Cade has been in town off and on dealing with Chloe. Yep, she won't give up. So far, he has gotten a restraining order so she can't come near me or him.

Come to find out, this isn't the first time that she has tried to track him down in the last couple years. *Can you spell psycho? I sure can.* She even tried calling the house after Cade changed his number, again. I kept yelling at her and then gave up answering the damn thing. Thank God for a little thing called caller ID.

Anyway, I'm basically stuck at the house, mainly in our bedroom. Cade insists on carrying me downstairs for meal times and drives me into town for my appointments. The last month has been hell …

"Fuck," I mutter as I lay my e-reader down and rest my head back against the headboard.

"Everything okay, sugar?" I look up to see Cade walking in with Timber. Man, my baby girl has grown.

"Oh, just great." I look down at my e-reader. "The guy I wanted the girl to be with turned out to be gay." I pout up at him as he starts to laugh.

"Poor baby." He fakes a pout then sits next to me. "Speaking of baby, how is my son?" He lifts my shirt and rubs my belly.

"Just like a couple hours ago, all's well!" I smile shaking my head. "What if the baby is a girl? Hmmm?"

"Then I'm going to be one protective daddy because she will be beautiful just like her mom." He kisses me sweetly. I miss those lips. He pulls away too soon, and I pout again. "Doctor said none of that until she gives us the okay."

"God!" I lay my head back again. "You have the patience of a saint!" Timber moves up the bed to me. I don't normally allow her up here but since I'm not allowed to go anywhere except the bathroom, I let her now. I grab her face and bring it to mine. She licks my nose. "Quit growing."

"Guess what?" Cade says coming out of the bathroom.

"Chicken butt," I say with a straight face. He just rolls his eyes. "What?"

"You get to leave the house today."

"Really!" I perk up. *Finally!*

"Well, I think your mom would be pissed at me if I kept you away on Thanksgiving." One of his brows arches up at me.

"Oh, shit ... I forgot." I usually make the dessert for dinner. Mom does the turkey; she refuses to let anyone touch her bird after it's plucked and cleaned. I am also usually the one who hunts it, but this year, with everything that happened, I'm not allowed to hunt again till after baby is born and someone goes with me. Cade got the honor of killing the bird, which sucks!

"Yeah, I figured you did when we got up this morning." He goes to the closet and starts to change. Hello, amazing sexy V on my equally amazingly sexy cowboy. I gawk, stare openly at him as he strips off one of his t-shirts and puts on a nice button up for dinner. *Drool.*

"Baby, get up and get dressed." He points to the *comfy* outfit he has for me. Fuck that shit, he dresses nice so do I.

I look out the window and see the wind is blowing snow everywhere. "I can actually get up on my own?" I challenge him just making him laugh and nod.

My Cowboy

I ease out of bed, placing my e-reader on my nightstand, and go to the closet to pick my own clothes out. No one has picked my clothes since I was little, even then I did it most of the time.

A nice pair of jeans and a deep v-cut long sleeve shirt will do. I pull my hair up in a nice ponytail, put on a little make-up, and I'm good to go. Only thing comfy that I will wear is my comfy boots. Cade hates them, says there is no traction and I'll fall in them, but I don't care.

"Ready." I bounce in front of him and watch as his eyes go straight for my chest. He then shoots a look up at me. Yep, that's what I was hoping for. "Come on, Cowboy. Mom hates it when anyone is late." I put my coat on and head to the truck with Timber and Cade hot on my heels.

~*~*~*~

I STARE OUT the window as Cade drives us home. No, staring isn't the right word, more like stewing and glaring. Timber's head is resting on my lap while I pet it.

Thanksgiving dinner at the Price household has always been interesting. Meaning someone usually either gets hurt or pissed off, and my mom is the one that usually gets pissed. When I was six, I convinced my cousin Steven to stick his head in the turkey, not cooked. He managed to get it stuck pretty good, and we had to take him to the ER to get it out. Mom was flaming.

When I was nine, Mom and I ran to the store to get something at the last minute. We told the guys, i.e. Cade, Tucker, Dad, and Nate, to watch the food and make sure nothing burned. The kitchen almost went up in flames because football was on. Again, Mom was mad.

When I was eleven, Cade and Tucker thought it would be nice for a change to fry the turkey, so they stole it and deep fried it. But when they were cutting it up, they got into a sword fight with the drumsticks, getting peanut oil everywhere, including in their eyes. They could barely see for the rest of the day. Once more, Mom was pissed.

And now, at the age of twenty-four, my boyfriend and baby daddy bulldozes my mom by saying she can't come in when we find out the sex of the baby but is allowed in the delivery room. And then demands that I marry him at the table. Yep, this year, *I'm pissed.*

I see the side of the road grow closer and closer. Shooting a look at Cade. "What the hell are you doing?"

"Ha. She speaks!" He glares back at me. "I'm pulling over."

"Well, I can see that. But, why?"

"You can't very well much move over to sit in your spot while the truck is moving can you?"

"And what makes you think I want to sit next to you right now?" I raise a brow challenging him.

"Get over here!"

Timber lifts her head then moves over to Cade's side. "Little traitor," I mutter as Cade laughs. I glare up at him. "I swear you're feeding her scraps."

"No, she just loves her dad." He pets her head then looks up at me. "Please come here," he pleads.

I cross my arms and just stare at him. He sighs then leans over to unbuckle me. He pulls me over to him, causing Timber to fall onto my lap then over to the spot I just left. "I'm sorry." He presses his forehead to mine while buckling me up next to him.

"You bulldozed my mom..." I just move my eyes to look up into his.

"I know. But the woman needs to learn that this baby," he moves his hand to my belly, "is my kid. I get a say so."

My Cowboy

I sigh but don't move my eyes. "It's her first grandchild."

"My...our first kid."

"Be nicer to my mom, please." I run a hand over his cheek.

"I'll try."

"And no demanding anything from me. You know I won't do it." I run my other hand over his other cheek. "Having your grandma throwing her wedding ring at me isn't what I want, either. I want something romantic to remember, not 'hey, remember when you demanded that I marry you and your grandma basically chucked her ring at my head.' Please." He nods. "And nothing on Christmas or New Year's. That is so tacky."

"I'll try." He kisses me softly on the lips. "I'm not giving up till you say yes."

He moves back to start driving again.

"Then this will be fun." I smile at him and rest my head on his shoulder. "I'm so happy that Tucker and Maddi are back together and *finally* getting married."

Cade keeps his eyes on the road but kisses my temple. "I'm glad he seems to be getting back to normal."

"Me, too." I cuddle into his side.

~*~*~*~

"EMMA." THE NURSE calls my name, drawing both Cade and me to look up. Today is my twelve-week appointment. Hopefully, Dr. Jen will say that I can get off bed rest because I'm really going crazy not being able to work.

Libby is doing well with her pregnancy. Otherwise, she is struggling. When Clint finally learned about her pregnancy, he told her to get rid of it to keep him. She told him to fuck off and hasn't seen him since. She has all of us, but I can imagine doing this alone while your best friend has her boyfriend has to be hard.

Blood pressure done, weighed and peed in the cup, and I'm ready to see the doctor. "I'm excited to see the baby again." I smile over at Cade, who has managed to fold himself into the tiny chairs in our room while I sit on the examining table kicking my legs.

Giving me his breathtaking smile, he says, "Me, too. Hearing his heartbeat is amazing, but I can't wait to see how big he's gotten." I roll my eyes. He still thinks baby is a boy.

There is a light knock, and Dr. Jen walks in. "Well, hello, you two." She beams us a smile. "How are you feeling, Emma?"

"She's driving me crazy," Cade mutters.

"I'm great, but I really am going crazy. Can I be off of bedrest yet?" I plead with her. "I'll only do light duty work." I point at Cade. "It's not like I don't have someone big and strong around the ranch who can do the heavy stuff for me."

She laughs while getting the ultrasound machine ready. "Well, let's take a look at baby and then I'll decide." She lowers the lights, and Cade comes to stand next to me.

Cade frowns as he watches her. "No alien finger?"

Dr. Jen smiles and laughs. "No, baby should be moved up a little higher since it is growing bringing Emma's uterus up as well so we can use the regular one now." She smiles down at me and turns the screen so we can see it better. "Ready to see the baby?"

We both nod. The screen comes to life as she puts the ultrasound on my lower stomach. Baby has gotten bigger. Instead of a little jelly bean, baby looks like a peanut. I feel tears come to my eyes as I see legs and arms moving back and forth like crazy.

My Cowboy

"Baby is really moving right now." Dr. Jen smiles and goes about measuring then turning on the doppler for the heartbeat. Like he always does, Cade pulls out his phone to record the baby's heartbeat. It warms my heart so much. He's going to be an amazing dad. The tears start to fall, and he bends down to kiss them away.

"I love you," I whisper to him.

"I love you, too."

"Well, baby looks great, and so do you, Emma." Dr. Jen pulls the ultrasound off and turns the lights back on while wiping my belly clean. "I'd say it's okay for you to go back to work. Light stuff, though."

I nod. "Don't worry, doc." Cade wraps me in his arms. "I won't let her do anything heavy. Driving the truck while we feed cows okay? The pastures can be bumpy."

"As long as she drives slow."

I smile. "I will."

"Umm ..." Dr. Jen and I look at Cade.

"Yes, Cade?" Dr. Jen asks.

"What about ... you know ..."

"What?"

He stumbles over his words until I jump in to save him. "Sex, he wants to know about sex."

"Oh!" She looks surprised. "Well, everything is fine for that. You go right at it." She now looks uncomfortable. "See you two soon." She flashes a smile and walks out.

I look over at Cade, who his smiling from ear to ear. "I'm going to rock your world tonight, baby."

"About damn time!"

Chapter Twenty

I HAVE NEVER been so thankful to be able to work again, even if I have to sit inside the cab of the truck while keeping my foot on the brake as Cade throws hay out the back.

This is fun. I am helping. I am contributing to my livelihood. A soft kick to my stomach draws my attention away from the mundane job of sitting in a truck that isn't even going at a snails pace.

"Daddy gets all the fun baby." I pat my belly. I can't wait to find out what we are having. Part of me wants to prove to Cade that this baby is *not* a boy just to rub it in his handsome face. I really don't care as long as he or she comes out with ten fingers, ten toes, two arms, two legs and a beautiful chubby little body with those cute chubby baby cheeks that make the lips pucker.

"Whoo!" The passanger door flies open and Justin hops in. I let Steven have a week off and forgot that we still needed help with feeding the cows. With it being a balming five below out with sharp winds, we needed another person to help Cade out.

So we have Justin. He and Cade have been taking turns sitting in the truck to get warmed up before going back out.

"It's colder than a witch's tit in a brass bra out there."

I snort a laugh and feel a dampness in my seat. *Fucking great.* Don't get me wrong, I love being pregnant but having my muscles slowly weaken down there sucks donkey butt.

"Well, get warmed up." I reach back and grab one of the five thermoses I brought, filled with hot coffee for the guys. "Here."

"Thanks." He graciously takes it and opens it up. "So....how's Libby?"

"Good, still pregnant and as feisty as ever." I smile widely at him. *I'm on to you, Foster.* It hasn't gone unnoticed by myself or Maddi, for that matter now, how Justin acts around Libby. That boy is in love and she is putting him through hell by not giving in to him.

"That's good..." He looks out the window while rubbing his gloved hands together. "Good."

"Why do you ask me about her every time I see you?" I cock a brow at him and let up on the brake when Cade taps on the window with the handle of the pitchfork.

"No reason. I'm just concern about my friend."

"She's a big girl, Justin. She can take care of herself."

"I know, but that fucking prick..." He shakes his head in rage. "He fucking left her, Emma. Pregnant! What kind of honorless asshole does that shit?"

I bark a laugh. "Coming from the guy who until recently was a total manwhore. What happened there?" I give him a pointed look. "You're in for a fight if you're after Lib."

"No," he basically shouts at me. "It isn't that, it's just...not that. My career."

"Your career?" I'm not buying this.

"Yes," He sounds like he is trying to convince himself as much as he is trying to convince me. "My career means so much to me right now. I can't reach the top if I'm chasing skirts around. I'm a reformed man."

"Right..." I'm cut off by Cade tapping on the back window again.

"My times up. Out I go." He smiles, relieved to escape me and my questions. *Until next time.*

~*~*~*~

TODAY IS THE big exciting day! January 24th, 2014 and we get to find out the gender of our baby. Last month, Libby found out her baby is going to be a boy. I'm so excited for her. I have a feeling my baby is a girl. But if I'm wrong, oh boy, her son and mine together are going to be a bad combination.

And even though Cade told my mom that she couldn't be there when we found out, she was still waiting out in the waiting room to be the first to know.

I had gone with Libby and her mom when she found out Dylan was going to be a boy. She picked that name because it goes for a boy or a girl, and she loves it. It was amazing to watch all the things the ultrasound could pick up on. I told Cade about it, making him even more excited.

Our lives have settled down, to say the least. As I hoped, Cade didn't try to propose on Christmas or New Year's. Actually, he hasn't even tried since Thanksgiving. And it's making me wonder.

As the screen comes to life, I have a hard time figuring out what we are looking at. I look up at Cade, and from his face, he also has a hard time. "That's baby's bottom," Dr. Jen answers our unspoken question. She points and moves her finger around the screen. "Back and there ..." she clicks and moves the ultrasound, "is the baby's head."

I look close and smile. "Baby has your nose." Cade smiles down at me. Sure does, my little ski slope nose.

My Cowboy

"I'm going to check everything out first if you're okay with this." She looks from Cade to me and back again. We both nod and watch her work and explain everything to us.

She points out the valves to the heart and watches the blood pump in and out of them. Legs and arms moving around. Even the baby putting a finger in its mouth. I start to tear up watching. *My little miracle.*

After about ten minutes of checking everything out, I think Cade is getting impatient. "When can we know what we are having?" He grinds his teeth. I slap his arm, and when he looks at me, I frown and mouth *behave*.

Dr. Jen laughs. "Okay. Ready?" Cade nods like crazy, and I laugh causing my belly to bounce and the ultrasound to move. It was enough movement that the baby crossed its legs and move the ultrasound. "Well, let me see if I can get the right angle." She starts to move it around with a frown but can't seem to get a good view. "Baby crossed its legs and is now covering up …" she mutters. She tries for a couple more minutes, but baby's legs refuse to move, completely blocking any view. She sighs and pulls the ultrasound off. "Sorry, you two, looks like baby wants to remain a secret a while longer." She turns the lights back on. "We'll try again, but baby is going to be growing so much it will get harder to tell." She shrugs.

I laugh and shake my head. Little miracle wants to surprise us, and I'm okay with that. Cade runs a hand through his hair then pulls his hat back now. "Damn." Then he smiles and shakes his head. "That's okay. As long as he's healthy." Dr. Jen laughs, tells us she will see us soon and leaves. "Stubborn like his mom."

He winks at me while I move to get off the table. I'm twenty weeks but look farther along since my frame is so small. Libby is about the same size at twenty-four weeks.

~*~*~*~

"I HATE HOW this dress looks on me." I smile over at Libby as I fix my own dress.

"You look fine." I come over and put my hands on her shoulders. "Just relax." *Easier said than done.* Libby may have grown use to being single and pregnant, but it doesn't make it any easier.

"It looked fine a month ago, now I just look like a marshmallow," she pouts. "A green one."

I pull her hair to the back then drape some on the sides. "Will you chill out. This is going to be a piece of cake. Besides..." I slap her butt, "you're not the only round one. And there is a reason why. We are pregnant." I go back over to my mirror and finish doing my make-up.

She huffs and continues to stare in the mirror. "I can't believe you couldn't find out what baby is." She changes the subject and moves to sit in one of the church chairs in the dressing room.

I shrug. "It's okay. I know my little miracle is safe and healthy; that's what matters." My hand goes to my belly, and I feel the baby kick me. Smiling, I look over at Libby. "I'll love it no matter what it is."

She smiles and rubs her own belly. I can see a quick jerk, meaning that Dylan just kicked her. "I feel the same. A long as he is healthy, I don't care."

I can still see that she is nervous, so I go sit next to her. "Everything will be fine." I kiss her cheek and the door opens.

My mom, Rebecca, and a very conservatively dressed Mrs. Beverley Barnett walk in. "Have you two seen the bride?"

I smile and walk into my mom's embrace. "Just using the shitter before getting in her wedding dress."

"Oh, Emma." My mom rolls her eyes, and Mrs. Barnett clears her throat.

I smile. "Sorry, but welcome to the family. Libby and I have quite the potty mouths."

"Darn right we do!" Libby kicks a leg up and down to get up. Round bellies and comfy chairs don't mix well.

Maddi walks out of the bathroom humming to herself then looks up and smiles at us all. "What?" she asks softly.

"Ready to get in your dress, dear?" Her mother *flows* over to her.

"Yes, Mother, I am."

Rebecca and my mom look at Libby and me. They see the green-eyed monster, wishing we behaved like that with them. Fat chance of that ever happening!

Once we have Maddi in her dress, the mothers clear out and in walks her dad. Boy, does that man command the room. Colonel Darrel Barnett is a force to be reckoned with and the one and only man to ever actually scare me.

Libby and I move out of the way and toward the door with our flowers in hand. "We'll give you two a moment," I whisper as I shut the door behind us.

"Man! That guy can scare the piss out of ya!" Libby says as we make our way down the hallway to where we are to wait.

"Not like that's too hard at the moment."

We both laugh as we stand there looking out into the church of all the friends and family that are there. There aren't a whole lot of people but just enough. Two-hundred is a big number. When I finally marry Cade, there will just be close friends and family, not everyone and their cousin like Maddi and Tucker.

"Don't you two look lovely." I turn to smile as my big brother comes walking up with Cade.

"Don't I know it; I get the honor of walking with both of them." Cade winks at me as he pulls me into his arms, kissing me fully.

I pull back and take them both in. Tucker is in his formal military gear or whatever you call it. He looks great. He proudly wears it with his hat tucked under his arm. He's all shaved and neat looking.

Then I turn to my cowboy. He's in a new pair of Wranglers with cleaned up boots and a mint green shirt on. His cowboy hat is in one of his hands. Oh, so sexy. Once Dr. Jen cleared me with everything, I can't seem to get enough of him. Oh, who am I kidding, I never got enough of him before getting pregnant.

I smile at both of them. The cowboy and the soldier. What a pair.

Tucker smiles and hugs me close. "Let's get this show on the road. Don't want you two on your feet too long." He kisses both Libby and me on the cheek and turns to our mom. "Ready, my beautiful mother?" He offers her his arm, and they move out into the church.

Cade closes the doors behind him and smiles down at me. I've become familiar with this smile the last few months. It's the one he gives me when he thinks about us getting married. "Soon, baby, soon," he promises.

"We'll see," I tease and bump elbows with him. Libby groans and rolls her eyes at us.

We hear voices coming down the hallway and see Maddi and her dad coming toward us. "She looks so beautiful," Libby whispers to me. I nod in agreement.

Maddi really does. She and Tucker both deserve this type of happiness.

She's beaming already. "You ready to become my sister?"

"I already am, but," she smiles at each one of us, "I'm ready to make it official."

Cade offers both his arms to Libby and I and readies us for our walk. He smiles down at both of us. "Yep, one lucky man."

As we walk down the aisle, I smile at familiar faces and even a few I don't know. We get a couple of weird looks from some older people in Maddi's family, probably because Cade is walking two pregnant women down.

From the corner of my eye, I watch Libby as we get closer to the front. Her walk falters a bit and I look to see what caused it.

When I see Justin sitting there smiling, I frown in confusion. She seems to recover and look away from him pretty quickly. *Interesting.*

Once we are to the front, Cade walks over to stand next to my brother while Libby and I take our spots on Maddi's side.

The doors open and Maddi walks in with her dad. All eyes are on her. Smiling, I see that she is glowing; she is extremely happy. I turn to watch my brother.

He looks like he did as a kid on Christmas morning. They deserve happiness and I really hope he can give it to her. I see a tear roll down his cheek, and I know that he's happy.

Maybe our lives are finally turning around for the better.

~*~*~*~

"YOU LOOK HAPPY." I lay my head on my brother's shoulder as we move side to side during our dance. Tucker wanted to have a special dance with just me to one of our dad's favorite songs.

"I am," he mutters, chin rested on the top of my head. "Really happy."

"I'm glad." I smile and play with part of his jacket.

"I never thought I would get here, especially after we lost Dad," he chokes.

"Me, too." I look up. "But he would want us to be happy, Tuck. He is up there watching over us, and even though we can't see him, we can feel him in the wind when the warm summer sun hits our skin, and someday in the eyes of all his grandchildren."

"When did you become so poetic?" He looks taken aback by my words.

I lift a shoulder. "I guess being so close to death it makes you look at things differently. I'm not scared to break down and cry now. I'm happy with myself and about to trust everyone again."

"Thank God." He hugs me tightly.

"Just teach your kids the lessons that Dad taught us and he'll be happy. Show them the love that he and Mom gave us and he will always be there and be proud of us."

"Good words of wisdom, little sister."

"It's what I do now," I brag. "I'm the glue." I gave up on telling anyone about my talk with my dad. Mom gets it and I think Cade does to a point, but I really needed that with him. I finally got the closure with my dad that I needed.

Chapter Twenty-One

AND HERE I thought I hated it that Cade got to get the turkey for Thanksgiving, but him getting the chance to get a mountain lion is *far* more annoying and torturous. *Damn snow in February.* I growl to myself.

"Knock it off; I wouldn't let you go even if it was nice out and you would walk the distances." I narrow my eyes up at Cade. He has a point; even if I could go, it isn't like I could shoot anything.

"Good luck." I kiss him at the door to the cabin where I am being dropped off along with our food, clothing and Timber. "Get the bastard that attacked me."

Laughing, he kisses my forehead before grabbing his pack. "I'll try. You two behave while I'm gone."

"Never." I tease, shutting the door behind him. I look down at my ever-growing belly and to my full-grown pup. "Well, you hungry?" I ask Timber. The baby kicks me hard, a sign that it is time to eat. "Okay, let's go whip something together." I pat my belly, only to be kicked again, and waddle my way into the main part of the cabin.

A slight chill hits me and I decide that it would probably be best if I start a fire first, so we don't freeze. Even with long johns under my maternity pants, a long sleeved shirt under my shorter one, a hoodie and a thick winter coat all topped off with the heat of pregnancy hormones, I'm still chilled.

After lighting the fire, I dig through the cooler to find the leftover chicken breasts from last night's dinner and heat them up along with some green beans.

Timber follows me around the small kitchen, whining for me to drop something. She has quickly learned that once something falls, there is no way that I can pick it up without ripping my pants.

Unfortunately for her, I don't drop anything this time around. After my food is ready, I plop myself onto the couch, kick my feet up and place my plate on my belly.

"Here comes some food, baby," I mutter around my piece of chicken. My little one gives me a light kick, causing a smile to erupt on my face. We sit quietly; well, almost quietly since Timber is still whining as I eat and watch the fire in a trance-like state.

I really hope that Cade is okay out there, I know he is a big tough guy but still ...

When I'm finished, I set my plate to the side. Timber jumps up and tries to lick my plate clean of anything I may have left her. When she finds no goodies, she looks up at me with that puppy pout. "Sorry." I try to have sympathy in my voice for her, but it fails. Cade is feeding her too many goodies to begin with and she's putting on weight.

I turn back to the fire while running my hands up and down my belly. I find myself doing this when I'm not sure what else to do. Sometimes, when I'm lucky, the little one will kick or hit my hands as they pass by. Right now, I can feel tiny little movements, but nothing major. Mommy is fed and now the baby is, too.

When I find myself alone, I usually talk to my little one; our one-on-one times have come to be very important to me. "Just a few more months and I will be holding you out here in my arms," I coo.

Thump.

"I can't wait to teach you things that I learned growing up."

Thump.

"How to ride a horse, rope, shoot, bait a hook, and well, throw a punch." I grin to myself and rub the spot I was just hit at.

Thump.

"I guess your dad can teach you those things too, but I'm better." I gloat. "Uncle Tucker is probably the best shot in the family though, so I may let him teach you."

Thump. Thump.

"Grandma will definitely be the one to teach you how to cook. I can get us by, but she is the master in the kitchen."

Taking a deep breath I lay my head back and stare up at the ceiling; the very same one that Tucker, Cade, Nate, and I helped my dad replace one summer after a tree came down and fell right on top of the roof.

"I wish your grandpas could be here to see you."

Thump.

"Grandpa Frank would be tough as nails on you, but would melt and do just about anything for you." A small tear comes to my eye. "You would have been his world just like Uncle Tucker and I were to him."

Thump.

"Then there's Grandpa Nate." I shake my head and smile. For two grown men, who had been friends their whole lives, you couldn't have found two people more opposite. "He would have been one of your best friends. He was always joking around and wore this weathered smile that warmed your heart. He was a great guy...they both were."

Thump.

"But even though they aren't here with us physically, they will always be with us spiritually. You'll never know them in your time on Earth, but you'll know when you feel them with you."

Thump.

"Yeah, baby, they are our angels now. But you still have a grandma and a great-grandma who will love you *so* much. Grandma Maggie will spoil you rotten!" The way I finish makes Timber bark and my little kicker stops moving. "Your great-grandma will be the one to teach you all the naughty things; that is, unless Aunt Libby gets to you first." The thought makes me laugh. Libby is going to have her hands full with her little one. I continue to rub my belly leisurely. I've seen that little light of spunk leave my best friend's eyes lately. She is changing; not that it isn't entirely a good thing. I love the sass and the feistiness that Libby has. Now she is focusing on the things that matter, but I think she is losing a part of herself to the change. I'm glad she is thinking about a career as a nurse, but I worry about her giving up on too much of her personality to protect herself from being hurt.

"We'll find a way to get her back."

~*~*~*~

DINNER IS JUST being set at the table when Cade walks in stomping his boots. He has a soured look on his bearded face. Yep, bearded. I wasn't so sure of it at first, but it has kind of grown on me. He says it keeps his face warmer when he is out working. I told him that was fine as long as it was gone by summer.

"Any luck?"

"Do I look like I killed something today?" he barks.

I bristle at him and narrow my eyes. "Just your attitude." I slam the last plate down. "Eat your fucking dinner and chill out." I seat myself and start digging in, not bothering to wait for him. *Grouch.*

Cade takes his time getting his gear off now that the cabin is warm and toasty from both the fireplace and the oven. "I'm sorry." He kisses my cheek before sitting in his place. "It was just a shitty day; the weather was bad and I didn't find a single sign."

"Okay," I murmur before taking a drink. "So you'll just try again tomorrow."

"Yeah." He cuts into his pork chop. "Let's talk about something more...exciting."

"Like?"

"Like..." He waves his hands around. "Baby names?"

"Baby names?" I ask dumbfounded. He wants to go from talking about hunting to baby names? "Okay, shoot."

"Well, for a boy I like Hunter Nathaniel, you know after our dads."

I nod, agreeing. "And for a girl?"

He stretches his head. "I thought I would leave that one up to you."

Again, I nod and start to think it over. And then it comes to me. "How about Aspen?"

Cade regards me for a beat. "Why Aspen?" he finally asks.

I take a minute to put myself together to say it. "I was..." *Breathe Emma. Breathe.* "The boys and I were in a grove of aspens when we were attacked."

Now I've confused him. "Why would you pick that name then?"

I shake my head out of frustration. "I don't expect you to understand, but because of that attack I got to see my dad one last time and it gave me a whole new outlook on life."

"Okay." Cade nods, reaching over and squeezing my hand. "Aspen if the baby is a girl. Middle name?" He goes back to his food.

"Miracle," I state. Cade's expression is one of complete surprise.

He swallows slowly, causing his Adam's apple to bob. "I love that."

"I thought you would." I smirk at him then go back to my food.

~*~*~*~

CADE AND I just were settled on the bench that Tucker made out of a fallen tree when Tucker, Maddi, and Libby pulled up. I thought since it was a scalding ten degrees out, it was perfect to have a little bonfire and having our friends and family show up is an added bonus.

"I'll head out with you tomorrow and see if we can find something," Tucker offers.

I'm about to dispute that trudging through the snow wouldn't be good on his leg, but Maddi catches me before my mouth opens. She slaps my shoulder and gives me a stern look. *Okay.*

"That would be great."

"Hell, yeah, it would," Libby speaks up. "That means you two won't be around to mess with us."

All of us, except Maddi, start laughing. "What am I missing?" Maddi leans over to ask me.

"These two," I point at Cade and Tucker, "had the nasty habit of trying to scare Lib and me when we were younger."

"Every time we were up here they would try to find a way," Libby added.

"Until the summer we were nine." I cuddle into Cade. His hand comes down on my belly. The look he gives me is one of complete admiration and love.

"What did you two do?" Maddi accusingly asks Libby and me.

"It wasn't our fault that they pretended to be bears while we were in our tent," I say defensively.

"They knew we had our BB guns in there with us."

Maddi looks bewildered and mildly entertained. "Those fuckers hurt when we got hit." Tucker rubs his arm, almost like he remembers the pain.

"I took most of them, dick-head," Cade growls at him. It's true, Tucker took off running like a scared little girl while Cade tried to calm us down and talk us into a truce with him.

"As I recall, you got us back the next morning." I elbow him in the side.

"So many ants." Libby stares into the fire and visibly shivers at the memory.

Maddi only shakes her head. "I'm *so* glad you all have grown up," she says sarcastically. She knows better.

Chapter Twenty-Two

I STRETCH AND open my eyes to see the early morning daylight pour out the window. I look up and see the early spring morning. I can't believe it's April already. And not just any day in April but April 15th.

No, not just tax day, but my birthday as well. Doesn't make for a fun birthday when you're rushing to get taxes done, but with Cade's help this year, I didn't live in the office.

I struggle to sit up and when I finally manage it, I look over to Cade's side which is made and his shorts are nicely folded on the side. Then I see a neatly folded paper on his pillow with my name on it.

Get dressed and head down to the room that nearly blew up. – I can't live without you.

I smile and quickly throw my hair up in a messy bun, pull on my jeans, socks, bra, and t-shirt. "Let's go find daddy, baby." I pat my belly and waddle my way down to the kitchen and see the breakfast waiting for me.

On the table is all my favorite foods; waffles with powder sugar, crispy bacon, strawberries and a tall glass of milk. I sit and take in the wonderful smell of my breakfast.

As I eat, I look up to see a vase filled with lilies, my favorite flower. And in the lilies is another note.

I read it while I continue to eat.

My Cowboy

Once you finish your meal, head to the place where we shared our first kiss. - I can't wait to share many more things with you.

Smiling, I quickly finish eating then grab my boots before heading for the back door. What? Thought it would be the living room? No, our actual first kiss happened when I was five years old, and he was nine. We were playing a game in the backyard by our swing that hangs off the cottonwood back there. I caught him off guard and went to plant one on his cheek, but he moved and I kissed him on the lips instead. We both found it gross.

I sit down on the swing and push my feet back and forth before I look over and see a note on the tree.

Inside this note is a piece of chocolate.

Now eat your chocolate and head to the place where the shit gets slick. - You mean the world to me.

Laughing, I take off out the side gate and head to the barn. The door is open, but it's quiet and dark inside. I turn on the light and start to look around. I see Ripper in his stall and go over to pet him.

He's been super jumpy. I really don't think I'll ever be able to put a saddle on him again, which makes me really sad. But I have decided it's for the best to stud him out. He would make great broncs for rodeo.

"Hey, boy." I quickly run my hand down his head before he shies away from me. I sigh sadly then move down to the stall where I fell in August.

On the side of the stall is another note with a bridle with it.

One last spot, sugar. Go to the spot where we shared our first 'bath'. - Love you.

This one I have to think over, but then I remember right after the shit incident we got into the little water fight and I ended up in the horse trough with him on top of me. Smiling, I make my way out of the barn and over to the corrals where it is located.

I come around the corner and freeze. Standing in the corral is the most beautiful black and white paint mare I've ever seen. She is standing there staring back at me as I slowly move toward her. She has a rope ribbon around her neck.

I put my hand out to let her smell me then she presses her nose to my hand. "Hey, beautiful." I look her over from my side. She's absolutely beautiful. She's mostly black with large white spots on her belly, hind end and around some of her legs and one of her eyes. "Beautiful," I whisper in amazement.

The light catches something that is on her ribbon, making me look down at it. There, on her ribbon, is a simple white gold band with a single stone in the middle. "Oh, my..." I cover my mouth as I feel tears start to fall and the baby move.

"Marry me, please," Cade's deep voice comes from behind me. I slowly turn around to see him in his work clothes and Muck boots down on one knee in front of me.

I suck a breath in. "Oh..."

"Please." He stands and walks to me. "Marry me."

I look back at the mare and then up at him. He has one arm wrapped around me and the other hand is on our baby. "Emma Jo Price. Please. Marry me," he whispers as he kisses the top of my head.

I nod, biting my lip. Words won't come. He pulls back and looks at me. "Yes?"

I nod again. "Emma, sugar. I need to hear you," he pleads.

I take a deep breath. "Y..." I'm still choking on my words. I calm down and beam the biggest smile I've ever had at him. "Yes. I'll marry you, Cade Nathan Masters." I start to cry again as he pulls me to him.

"God! I love you." He lifts me into his arms and kisses me soundly on the lips. Then he swipes his tongue across my mouth before I open to him. I grab the hair on both sides of his head fusing him to me even more. It's not a sweet, passionate kiss; this is a sex-crazed, madly in love, I'm going to consume you like a coyote would a baby lamb kiss. *Not a completely pretty sight.*

We finally pull apart and catch our breaths, and he smiles against my face. "I love you," I whisper as I run one of my hands over his lips.

"I love you." We both turn to look at the mare. "She's yours."

I look back at him in shock. "Really?"

He nods. "That's what I've been up to. That's why I was gone for the last couple days. Had to drive clear to Bozeman to get her."

I slide out of his arms and walk over to her. "Her name?"

"Vamp." I shoot a questioning look at him. "Don't know." He shrugs.

"She's beautiful." I run my hand through her mane.

"Just like you. I know you would probably never be able to get on Ripper again, so I thought I should get you one you could ride." He comes up and wraps his arms around me resting one hand on top of my belly and the other on the bottom, hugging our child.

I look up over my shoulder to him and kiss his cheek. "She's wonderful. Thank you." I kiss him again and look back at my new horse.

Now the next two and half months need to hurry and get here so I can ride her after baby comes.

I'm not given anymore time to admire her when I'm lifted into the air like a feather by Cade. "What are you..." Cade cuts me off by sealing my lips with his. His tongue licks the seam of my mouth waiting for acceptance into my mouth. He is cradling me in his arms, so I turn my upper body the best I can to lock my hands together behind his neck.

I open my mouth and lap at his tongue, welcoming him in. It's times like these when I'm in his arms that I don't feel like a bloated heifer. He makes me feel small, cherished, and loved.

The mud under his Muck boots sloshes as he carries us across the driveway and up to the house. I'm barely aware of the fact that we are walking around the side of the house until I hear the gate squeak open and then closed.

"Where are we..." I break our kiss only as he lowers me onto the washing machine and begins to rain kisses down my neck and over the top swell of my chest. All the while removing his coat and undoing his belt before moving to my maternity pants.

"I want you, sugar." His hot breath ignites the passion within me, turning me on. Thankfully, my pregnancy likes sex lots of sex. So much more that Cade barely has to touch me and I'm pooling in my panties, dripping and oh so ready for him to consume me. "You ready for me?" He looks down into my eyes. His concern melts me. Even though we have been given the all clear to have fun, Cade still goes slow and never pushes me too much. He doesn't want anything to happen to me or our baby.

"Yes," I pant. I lift myself to quickly kick off my pants and edge myself forward.

Cade makes quick work of getting himself free and ever so slowly lowers me onto his hot, pulsating erection. We groan together as he fills me completely. "Heaven," he mutters, eyes closed and head tilted up.

I dig my hands into his strong biceps and hold on for the slow, love-filled ride that he gives me against the washing machine. Cade pulls out as slowly as he goes back in. I feel every single inch of him work its way both in and out of me.

This is nothing like the sex we had before my pregnancy and my accident. Fast, furious, and explosively passionate love was before and I miss it, but I love this way just as much. We take our time, loving one another, holding onto each other. In a way, this feels so much more intimate as we watch each other get closer and closer to the release we can only get from one another. "I love you," I manage to say as he slides back into me, filling me perfectly.

"And I love you." He cups my face, knowing that I'm safe between him and the washing machine.

I lick my lips and try my best to grip him tighter. It is getting harder the closer I get to my due date. "I'm there, Cade."

"Let go, Emma," Cade instructs just as I feel him surge forward once and then still himself. His mouth hangs open as his eyes flutter closed.

My orgasms this way are different as well. Sweeter and come more steadily but still as intense. "Cade," I breathe against him as I kiss his stubble covered face. Our own brand of perfect love was made in the laundry room against the washer with most of our clothes still on including his Muck boots. Life couldn't get more wonderful.

Chapter Twenty-Three

MY BEST FRIEND is a mommy. I smile to myself as I waddle my way back into Libby's post partum room. She's sound asleep. The excitement of getting to the hospital along with delivering Dylan took it out of her.

Rebecca left with me a few hours ago. She needed to get back to Lee to make his dinner before he went off to work for the night. Maddi had left with Tucker since she didn't have a ride home. And I ran to my mom's house for a quick nap.

"How's my nephew," I sing into the room, finding it dimly lit and Libby still sound asleep.

"You just missed her." Justin's voice takes me by surprise.

"You're still here? Or did you just get back?" I look over to find Justin sitting in the rocking chair holding the little blue bundle that is Dylan.

"I never left." He doesn't look up at me, he just watches Dylan. "Isn't he amazing?"

"Like his momma," I say with pride as I walk over and look down over Justin's shoulder just as Dylan yawns. "Someone else looks ready for bed." I run a finger over his soft chubby cheek.

"Libby just fed him and crashed again," Justin explains.

"And you got to stay for that?" I ask in almost disbelief. My best friend has been skirting around her feelings for Justin for a while now and with her stubborn attitude I don't see it changing any time soon.

"No." Justin laughs. "She made me put the curtain up between us while she fed him."

The room falls into silence. I want to ask if I could hold him, but now that Dylan is falling asleep, I don't want to disrupt him. Besides, the look of wonder and love in Justin's eyes is pretty amazing to see.

"Isn't he amazing?" Justin asks again. *He must really love Dylan.* Justin thankfully got Libby to the hospital in time to deliver and stayed through the whole thing. I, for one, thought he would have run screaming, but he stayed by Libby's side the whole time.

I know if she would just let him in, Justin would be good to both her and Dylan.

"Like his mom," I repeat my answer. "But you already know that, don't you?"

"For a long time," he answers me quickly.

~*~*~*~

"COME ON, EMMA, one more push!" Cade holds my hand as I bear down and push.

Libby reaches ten, and I fall back on the bed trying to catch my breath. "You can do this, Emma. Baby is so close." My mom pushes my hair off of my forehead and places a kiss there.

"You made this look so easy." I glare over at Libby.

"It's called an epidural, my dear." She grins. *Fuck her.* "I got here right as my pains started getting closer and were able to get one. Not my fault you waited until your water broke to come here, only to find out you are already dilated to eight."

I take a deep breath and grab my mom and Cade's hands again. Libby starts her counting again as I push.

My Cowboy

"Good. Good. Emma, I see the head." Doctor Jen smiles up at me. After I reach ten again, I fall back.

"Come on, Emma, one more push, sugar." Cade kisses my forehead, and I scowl at him.

"One more push? You're fucking kidding me!" He stands back shaking his head and laughing. "You can do this next time!" I feel the urge to push again.

I've been in labor for about twelve hours now. I've only known I was for about the past four hours, though. After my accident, pain isn't too bad to handle, but pushing a kid out hurts.

I push for the next five minutes when the head is finally out. "Okay, Emma. I need you to stop so I can clean the baby's head up and clear airways." Doctor Jen makes quick work of that. "Okay, one more push Emma." I bear down and push and then it's gone. The pain, it's gone. Doctor Jen looks up at me to Cade, my mom, Libby, and back to me with a smile. "It's a girl."

I start to cry as Cade moves down to cut our daughter's cord. They quickly go to work cleaning her up and handing her over to the baby doctor.

Doctor Jen turns back to me. "Lucky you, you didn't tear. But you do need to just push out the placenta. It will be easy." I nod and start to push when she tells me. She quickly cleans me up then I'm allowed to hold my baby girl.

I look over to see the nurses working on making sure she's fine, and Cade watching with tears in his eyes.

"Eight pounds, ten ounces." One of the nurses announces her weight. "Twenty-one inches." Her length. The nurses continue to call numbers while Doctor Jen instructs me to take off my top so my daughter can get skin to skin comfort with me and to see if she needs to feed.

After about ten minutes, Cade walks over to my bed with our tiny little girl in his massive arms. "Ready to meet our daughter, sugar?" I nod and reach for her. He kisses her on the top of her head and hands her to me.

She's awake and looking right up at me with the darkest eyes I've ever seen, making me smile. "She has her daddy's eyes." Cade sits on the side of the bed wrapping both of us in his arms.

"Her name?" the nurse asks.

I look down at her as she tries to find my breast for her meal. "Aspen Miracle Masters." I kiss her head and try to get her to latch on to me.

"Okay. Aspen Miracle Masters born at 7:45 p.m. on June 6th, 2014," the nurse rattles off as Cade and I watch our daughter.

"I love you," Cade whispers into my ear. I lean into him.

"I love you, too." He kisses me sweetly before getting up.

"Better go make some phone calls." He kisses both of us once more then leaves.

Libby comes walking back into the room and takes a seat at the foot of the bed. "Thanks for the help, Lib."

"Anytime." She smiles. "I think she'll be blond like you."

"You think?" I look down at Aspen as she looks back up with me. "Brown eyes and blond hair, she's perfect."

"Oh, no." I look up at Libby, who is now frowning. "What?"

"Dylan and Aspen…" She shakes her head.

"What?"

My Cowboy

"They are going to be little demons." She laughs and shakes her head again. A look comes across her face as she thinks of the trouble our children will be in together.

"Just like their moms." We both look up to Cade as he makes his way back into the room.

"Damn straight." Libby smiles. "So, wedding plans? How are those coming?"

"She gets a month then she's mine."

"Well, then." Libby gets up, making me frown in confusion. "I've got a party to plan. Love ya guys! Congrats!" She walks out the door.

I look up at Cade, who only shrugs, then smiles down at Aspen, who has fallen asleep. His hand looks like a giant's hand next to her head. "She's perfect."

Smiling, I pull her from me and kiss her head. "Yes, she is."

~*~*~*~

"SHE'S SO TINY." Maddi holds her niece close to her as she moves to the chair in my room. "Oooh." She kisses her head and looks back up at me then to Tucker.

"Uh-oh, I know that look." I smile at my brother.

"Tucker...I want one," she pouts.

Glaring down at me then turning back to his wife, he smiles and nods. "Not my fault she wants one. Give me a niece or nephew to teach naughty things to." I stick my tongue out at him as he moves to sit next to Maddi.

He smiles down at Aspen. "You did good, sis." Kissing her head then his wife, he smiles at me.

"I do the best I can." I watch as they fuss over my daughter and smile at seeing them both so happy. They've come a long way from where they were a year ago. "So, any plans on moving out of Mom's?"

Tucker looks up from Aspen, who is now in his arms. "No, we thought that staying with her would be good for her."

"We don't think she's ready to be all alone yet," Maddi finishes.

I nod. "Good thinking."

"So, wedding plans?" Maddi tucks some of her hair behind her ear. "Have you found a dress yet?"

"Yep, and it screams me."

"Why? Does it have camo on it?" Tucker snorts a laugh, causing Aspen to start to fuss.

I take her back with a shit-eating grin. "Actually, yes, it does. It's mostly white, though, the bottom is camo, laces up in the back and strapless. I fell in love with it the moment I saw it."

"Does that mean we are in camo as well?" Maddi frowns.

"Yep." I pop the 'p' and grin. "Don't worry, you and Lib will look lovely." I wink then kiss my daughter.

"Cade, too?" Tucker laughs.

"Yes." I glare at him. "And you, too, mister."

"Fuck that." He stands up then holds a hand out to Maddi so they can leave. "I'll wear what I wore to my own wedding. At least it's green." He smiles. "See ya later, sis."

"Bye, you guys."

~*~*~*~

ASPEN HAS BEEN with us now for two whole weeks! She is such a good baby. She is only waking a couple times at night and doesn't fuss like I thought babies did. Libby says I'm lucky; Dylan fusses a lot.

Tonight is the night of my party with Libby and Maddi. We aren't good at making friends with many girls, so we decided just to have a girls' night at my house for the

My Cowboy

evening while Cade hung out with Tucker at my mom's with Aspen.

Libby pretty much has everything figured out but needed me to get a few things from the store. So, after dropping Aspen off for grandma time before Daddy gets there, I get to the store to get the last couple of things on Libby's list.

Cade has been busy himself getting things arranged for the rodeo camp. He's also helping me prepare the bulls for a few rodeos. We won't start the camp till next year but getting us geared up with stock doesn't hurt.

Ice Cream-any flavor. Libby has written down as the last thing on her list.

As I pull the ice cream out of the freezer, I turn to see Chloe standing down the aisle from me glaring. *Great.*

I do my best to ignore her and make my way past her, but she just had to open her trap. "And you thought I looked bad after having Wyatt. Ha! No wonder Cade's been calling me." This I know is a lie. My grip on my cart tightens until my knuckles turn white. "Fucking fat-ass," she hisses.

I glare up at her and grind my teeth. "At least I can fit into my pants normally. You forced your pants and on now it looks like two rock dogs fighting in a gunny sack as you walk." I start to walk away when I feel my ponytail being tugged.

"Stupid bitch, you took him from me!" she screams as she turns me around. I really don't take the time to talk this over. For all I know, she will be throwing a punch at me.

My first instinct is to hit her. So, I do. One fist to the nose and she goes down screaming.

The next few minutes kind of shock me because we are both put in handcuffs.

"Can I make my phone call please," I ask the officer once we get to the jail. He guides me to the phone. I glare over at Chloe as I walk over. "Better get out of town. Next time they probably wouldn't be able to recognize you," I whisper making her eyes grow.

"Emma Jo Price, will you behave yourself." I look up to see Lee walk in.

"Afternoon, Lee...I mean Sheriff Vance."

"Make your phone call." He nods to the phone.

I take a deep breath and dial Cade's number. "Hello?" His rough voice comes over the phone sending chills up my back. "Hello?"

"Hey, cowboy."

"Emma?"

"Yep." I play with the cord to the phone.

"What number are you calling me from? Why not your cell?" He's concerned. "Is Aspen okay? Are you okay?"

"She's fine, still with mom, but I need you to come get me ... and bring the checkbook," I mutter.

"What happened, Emma?" Now, he sounds concerned AND pissed.

"Well, I'm sort of at the...jail."

"What did you do!" I cringe at his voice.

"Got into a fight at the store with Chloe."

I hear him sigh, and I know that he is rubbing a hand down his face. "Okay. Give me a few and I'll be in to get you. Jesus, woman."

"Love you."

"Love you, too." We hang up, and I go back to sit in the chair by the officer's desk.

"How is it fair! That bitch hit me first. Why isn't she in a cell?" Chloe yells at Lee.

My Cowboy

"Because I know she won't run off," is all he says. I smile.

~*~*~*~

"THAT IS HILARIOUS!" Libby laughs from her spot on the couch.

"Yeah, well, Cade was pissed." I take another handful of popcorn and sit back again. "Even though he did laugh after we left and got my truck."

"Emma, will you ever learn?" Maddi shakes her head at us as she turns back to the movie. We decided on a movie and snack night. Libby and I are both nursing and, Maddi is trying to get pregnant so we can't drink. And since I already visited the jail today, going out wasn't in the works.

"Nope." I smile. I know just what she is talking about. After I had discovered Trey was cheating on me, I got into a fight at the bar with Lilly that night. I didn't get arrested mainly because I only threatened her with a baseball bat.

"So, just so you know." We turn to Libby. "If I ever get married, I want a passion party for my party."

"Passion party?" Maddi asks with a frown.

I shake my head. "She means that she wants to have sex toys on display to buy for her party." I laugh, turning back to the movie. Maddi sits there bright red and stunned.

After the movie, I show the girls their bridesmaid dresses. "Camo? Seriously?" Libby groans as she lays back.

"What?" I glare at her. "They are short and sexy and just your style. Deal with it." I punch her in the leg.

"Aspen going to be in camo as well?" Maddi asks looking over the dress and nodding.

"Yep, and I even found her a little cream colored diaper cover that has camo ruffles on the bottom." I smile and show them the picture of the dress that my little girl will be wearing.

"You and camo." Libby shakes her head but grins. "But since I love you, I'll wear it."

"Good because I will rope you and force the damn dress on you."

We all start laughing, but seriously, I would do it.

Chapter Twenty-Four

I TAKE A deep breath and pull the dress over and smile down at Aspen. "Who's the most beautiful little girl," I coo at her. She looks up at me with her big brown eyes. She isn't to the point of smiling yet, but she knows her momma's face.

I pick her up and smile again. Her thick, curly, light blond hair is pulled back with a camouflage headband and her camouflage dress. Aspen is the cutest little girl in the whole world.

"Doesn't she look precious?" My mom claps her hands together and reaches for her grandbaby. "Come to Grammie, sweetie." She takes her from me. "All fed?" I nod. "Okay." She kisses Aspen's head. "Let's let Mommy and your aunts get ready." Mom and Aspen head for the door. "We are going to go find Uncle Tucker, who I believe has Dylan and maybe daddy and great-grandma."

After they leave, I turn back to Maddi and Libby. "Let's get to it." Our hair and make-up are all done, and they are already dressed, which just leaves me. I had to nurse and pump before I could finish getting ready. I head to my bedroom from Aspen's room and put on the little number I bought for tonight. I get my dress on and brace myself against the wall. "Do me up, baby," I wink at Libby as she moves to start lacing up the back of my dress.

"Nervous?" Maddi asks as she helps hold my sides as Libby tightens my dress.

"Never...well, maybe a little." I gasp. "Damn, Jones! Not so rough!"

"Quit moving then or I'll start pulling your hair, too." She sets back to working on my back and when I'm all done, I run my hands down my sides and turn to the mirror.

"You look amazing, Emma." Maddi smiles as she fixes my long curled hair. "Would never guess you had a baby a little over a month ago."

I laugh and flex my arms. "Ranch work is the best workout." It's true. After Aspen was born, I got my butt in gear to get work done and lose the little baby weight that I had gained. I wanted to look amazing for Cade today.

"I can't believe after today you two will be wives." Libby smiles, but it's a sad smile.

"You'll get there someday." I wrap her in a hug then grab Maddi and bring her in, too. "Just need someone who will put up with your crazy ass." We all laugh until we hear a throat being cleared.

We look toward my door to see Tucker standing there waiting. "Glad to see you aren't trying to sneak off to find Cade."

We laugh again. "No, she tried that last night," Maddi said moving to her husband. He smiles down at her before wrapping her in a tender hug followed by an equally tender kiss. "Love you."

"Love you, too, Angel." He looks back at me. "Ready to become Mrs. Masters?"

"Hell, yeah!" We grab our flowers white lilies, of course and head for downstairs.

The wedding is being held in our backyard. I thought it would be nice since it is just a small wedding and my yard is huge. We have a tent set up for dinner with a dance floor and all.

My Cowboy

Once in the kitchen, we get lined up. Mom is walking down with Aspen in one arm and Dylan in the other. Timber is already out there somewhere with her camo bow on; she's probably sitting next to Cade. Maddi is next, and then Libby. Once they head out, the doors close, and I take a deep breath.

Tucker takes my arm. "I wish Dad was here." He smiles down at me.

I smile back at him. "He's right here." I point to his heart and mine. "He's always with us," I whisper before closing my eyes and taking another deep breath. "I love you, Dad," I whisper before the doors open, and we head out.

I look up once we are down the two steps of the back porch. Everyone is smiling, standing facing Tucker and me. My breath catches when I look down at the end to where the love of my life stands smiling holding our baby girl.

He's in a camouflage button up that shows off his muscular body very well, making me drool. He's in a new pair of Wranglers and his same old work boots and belt. He even cleaned his black Stetson up to make it look nice for today.

I smile at him as I get closer, and as I figured, Timber is in her spot right next to his feet.

When we reach them, I try to keep going to be in his arms, but Tucker pulls me back making everyone laugh. "Who gives this woman to this man?"

Tucker stands up tall and strong. "Our mother..." he smiles down at me, "myself, and our father give her." Tucker takes my hand in his shaking one and passes it to Cade's outreached one. He kisses me on the cheek then turns to sit with my mom and Maddi.

"Hey," I whisper to Cade.

"You look stunning." He smiles down at me before shifting our daughter in his right arm. We turn to the pastor with smiles.

"Today, on this beautiful day, we are here to witness the union of these two. Cade Masters and Emma Price." I take a deep breath just as the wind picks up and blows around us. *Dad.* He turns to Cade. "Do you, Cade, take Emma to be your lawfully wedded wife? To love and cherish, in sickness and in health, as long as you both shall live?"

Cade smiles down at me. "I do."

"And do you, Emma, take Cade to be your lawfully wedded husband? To love and cherish, in sickness and in health, as long as you both shall live?"

I bite my lip, nod, and smile up at Cade. "I do."

"They have decided to say their own vows." The pastor turns to me. "Emma."

I turn and look up into Cade's eyes and reach up with my free hand to place it on Aspen's back. "I have loved you for a long time, Masters." My eyes tear up, and I give a nervous laugh. "You were the first boy I ever kissed and the first one to steal my heart. Then you left us, and I was broken. I thought my feelings for you would go away but even after ten years…eleven now, I still feel the same way for you that I did when I first thought of you as more than a boy with cooties." A little laughter goes out. "Then you came back after all the torment that went on in my life." I look over at my mom and Tucker. "My brother's injuries and my father's death." I look back at him and wipe the tears threatening to fall from his eyes. "You saved me. You helped me." I touch Aspen once more. "You gave me a sense of belonging and two people worth living for. I love you, Cade, no matter what." I shake my head and feel tears fall. "I'm so excited I finally get something I've always wanted…you."

My Cowboy

I take a deep breath and smile through my happy tears up at Cade. "Well, monster, you get your wish." His voice booms with emotion making everyone laugh. "I always knew that you had a crush but knowing that I have your love is an incredible feeling." He kisses Aspen's head. "I was lost for a long time before I found my way back home. Never in a million years would I have expected to see a beautiful, strong amazing woman who would capture my heart and fill the emptiness in my soul." He wipes my tears away. "Knocking you with the barn door was the best thing to ever happen to me. Seeing a beautiful woman cussing her head off was amazing. Then when you looked up into my eyes, I could finally breathe again." He holds my hand tightly. "You became my reason for living, for staying, for loving." He kisses Aspen again. "You gave me a beautiful daughter who I will cherish and love as much as I do you. I can't wait for the years to come and what life will bring us. I love you, Emma."

"I love you, too, Cade," I whisper, choking on all the emotion I never knew I could handle.

We turn back to the pastor. "The rings." Libby being herself, of course, pulls the rings out of her cleavage and hands them over to us causing everyone to burst out laughing. Looking at Cade, the pastor says, "Repeat after me. With this ring, I thee wed."

Cade slides the ring on my finger. "With this ring, I thee wed."

He looks at me. "And the same with you, Emma. With this ring, I thee wed."

I grab his hand with both of mine and slowly slide the ring on him. "With this ring, I thee wed."

"Now you may kiss your bride." Cade leans down, scooping me up close to his chest and kisses me deeply. "I proudly present in front of all you witnesses and the good

Lord himself, Mr. and Mrs. Cade Masters." We kiss Aspen together then turn to our friends and family.

"You're finally mine," I whisper up at him.

"And you, mine." He kisses me again as we walk down the aisle and over to the tent.

~*~*~*~

AFTER PICTURES, DINNER, cake, and dancing, we make our way around the tent to visit with everyone who is still here. I'm talking with my mom and Rebecca when Cade pulls me into his arms. "Dance with me, Mrs. Masters."

I smile up at him, cupping one cheek while kissing the other. "Okay."

"Hey, I want a dance!" We turn and see Libby storming toward us.

"Fine." Cade frowns but doesn't move to let go of me.

"Not you, Masters." She smiles at me. "My sexy bitch." She winks.

"Where's Dylan?" I look back at Rebecca, but she doesn't have him. My mom has Aspen and Maddi is dancing with Tucker.

"Cumdrop has him." She points over her shoulder.

"What?" Cade asks the same time I say.

"Who?" Libby-isms, you never get used to them.

"Cumdrop." She huffs and rolls her eyes. "Justin." We both lean to our right side to look over her shoulder seeing Justin trying to figure out how to hold Dylan and frowning, only making him cry. "Crap. Be right back." Libby turns around and stomps up to them and shows Justin how to hold him properly.

Cade shakes his head and pulls me with him. "Libby and her weird names for things."

"Yeah." I wrap my arms around him as we start to sway. "First vagina hugs now cumdrop."

"Your mom is taking Aspen tonight right?" I nod into his shoulder. "Good because I'm going to love you all night long."

That got my full attention. My core starts to warm. "Well, it's our party. We can leave whenever we want." I raise my eyebrows at him and bite my lip.

"Fuck..." he draws out. "Party's over!" Cade yells causing everyone to stop what they are doing and stare at us.

"Cade," I groan as I bury my reddening face into his chest.

A long two hours later, my mom is the last one to leave with Aspen. I really don't want my baby away all night, but I know she is in good hands. After Cade forces me into the house, he picks me up and carries me to our room.

"Now for our own brand of fun." His voice is filled with lust and love, making my body warm up.

"Just let me get this dress off." I turn my back to him. "With your help."

"Gladly." He makes quick work of my dress. Once it pools at my feet, I turn to face him again. "I am one lucky man." He looks me up and down while taking off all his clothes in a hurry.

Once he's stripped, he charges me, lifting me into his massive arms and throwing me on the bed making me giggle. I sit up on my elbows as he crawls up to me, taking my lips in a rush. He holds my left hand in his right one and moves his left hand down my side until he reaches my tiny strap of underwear. He pulls back a tiny bit. "Baby, as much as I love this outfit, it's in the way." He rips it clean off of me. He slides his fingers into my folds and presses against my clit, making my head fall back and a moan escape me.

He moves his mouth to my neck as he circles my clit then plunges two fingers into me. He hooks his fingers up and to the left causing me to scream and push my hips up into his hand. "That's it, baby. Ride my fingers." Quickly, I fall over the edge, grabbing a strong hold of his upper arms, digging my nails into him and screaming his name.

Before I can even calm down, he thrusts quickly into me jarring me and moving me up the bed a little. "Fuck! Cade!" I throw my head back then look up into his eyes. "I love you," I pant after my second orgasm rocks through me.

He pulls out slowly then thrusts quickly back in. "I love you, too." He continues to pound in and out of me then moves one hand from my hip to my clit pressing and circling it. I don't know what is different about tonight, but my third orgasm hits me hard and fast.

"Oooooohhhhh ... Ooooo Cade!" I meet his thrusts with my own making him groan as well. I grab hold of his arms again and hold on because there isn't anything else I can really do.

"Milk me, baby." My fourth orgasm hits me hard making me clamp down on him pushing him over the edge. "Emma!" he yells as he goes feral for a moment then calms down.

Covered in sweat and breathing hard, he slowly pulls out and lays next to me. I move to my side facing him and wipe some sweat off of his brow. "I love you."

"I love you." He pulls me into his arms where sleep quickly finds me. I'm so glad that I'm at this point in my life, with an amazing husband, a precious daughter, and knowing that my life is right where it should be. I thank God for being knocked in the face by that barn door.

Epilogue

5 Years Later...

I STAB MY pitchfork into the stack of crap and hay that I've made after mucking the stalls in barn two. Removing my baseball cap, I wipe my brow and look around to make sure that I managed to clean everything.

My checklist is done for the day, it seems. I take the wheelbarrel out and dump the load looking over to see Libby putting barrels away from the barrel racing lesson that she gave an hour ago in her own little arena. While Tucker is giving roping lesson to a bunch of kids.

Smiling, I make my way over to the rough stock arena. I can hear cheering coming from there. I walk around the back of barn one and see the cutest thing in the world and something that I will never tire of. Little kids lined up along the fencing, watching Cade riding one of the bulls, teaching and showing the older kids at our rodeo camp what to do.

I walk up behind the little kids crossing my arms and watch my sexy cowboy going to town on Roundhouse.

"Go Daddy! Go! Get him!" I smile down at Aspen as she climbs the side of the fence cheering her dad on.

"Go ga! Go! Him! Him!" Laughing I bend down and pick up my little boy.

"Wanna see Daddy better, little man?" Two-year-old Hunter grins at me and nods his head like crazy. Cade says that Aspen is my mini me, she's just like her mom, but I think she's starting to get Aunt Libby's attitude. But Hunter is all his daddy looks, attitude, everything. I kiss his cheek then turn back to Cade, who has now dismounted.

"Great job, Uncle Cade!" Dylan is up on the fence with Aspen. Partners in crime, those two. You see one, you get the other and a whole bunch of trouble. At least I know Dylan will always protect Aspen. Best example; he killed a rattlesnake with a garden spade at my mom's house just a couple months ago. Kid didn't even blink, just did it because it scared Aspen.

Cade instructs some things to the older kids after Roundhouse is put in his pen.

I walk up and kiss Aspen on the back of the head. "Cheering for Daddy?"

She bats her blond hair out of her face and smiles up at me with bright red cheeks. "Yep! Did ya see him, Mommy! Daddy is the best bull rider in the whole wide world!" She bounces on the fence.

"I don't know about that, baby girl."

"Daddy!" Aspen hurries up to finish climbing the fence to get to her dad. "You're the best!" She wraps her little arms around his neck and gives him a big kiss on the cheek. Yep, she's daddy's little girl.

"Yeah, Daddy, you're the best." I smirk at him before I kiss him on the lips.

"Gross!" Aspen buries her face in Cade's shoulder as we continue to kiss.

"Hey, sugar." Cade pulls back just a little and gives me the look, the one that makes me want to send the kids on their way so we can be alone.

"Behave." I shake my head at him before kissing him one more time.

"And what did little man think of Daddy's ride?" Cade kisses Hunter's cheek.

"Ga!" Hunter launches himself out of my arms over the fence to his dad.

Cade laughs as he grabs him. "Looks like I'm the superhero today."

Turning around and heading to the house smiling, I say, "Dinner will be done after a bit. Kids' parents should be here soon."

"'Kay, sugar."

~*~*~*~

LATER THAT NIGHT, I sit on the back porch watching Cade chase our kids around the yard with Timber playing as well.

I sip my tea and feel the light breeze come from the hills. "Thank you for sending them to me, Dad," I whisper.

Looking down at Cade on the ground with Aspen and Hunter falling on him, all laughing, I couldn't imagine my life any better. I am truly blessed. I have an amazing husband who can give me children. I rub my ever growing baby bump. At the moment, I have two amazing children who make my life worth everything, and soon, a third little one chasing his brother and sister around along with their cowboy dad.

Price and Masters Rodeo School is doing great, bringing more and more kids in for the last four years. We have helped many kids have the opportunity to get into rodeo and do really well.

Masters Rodeo Company is in full bloom; Roundhouse was just retired as a top-ranked bull in the U.S. I have many more bulls and broncs that are doing great. Several of Ripper's children have become very sought after because they are amazing broncs.

And as for the ranch as a whole, well, we do well. I know that as long as we work hard, we will never suffer or be in the red again. Cade coming back into my life was the best thing that happened to my home.

Not a day goes by that I'm not thankful for everything in my life and how well everything seemed to work out.

Life will always be amazing as long as I have my cowboy by my side.

THE END

Bonus: Cade's POV

Re-Meeting Emma

I DON'T KNOW what in the world possessed me to stay away from this place for so long. Shaking my head as I park my truck next to the barn I get out and stretch my legs.

Damn that was a long ride. Looking around, little has changed here in ten years. Only difference now is that it is really quiet around here.

I can see some horses out in the fields and hear some moving around in the barn. "Anybody here!" I yell and wait. No answer. I grab my hat from the seat and pull it on.

"Well what the hell?" I walk around the main house and the other structures around the place. It doesn't look like anyone has been around all that often. *Again what the hell?*

I decide to go check out the barn, walking in two heads lift up out of a couple of weathered stalls. "This place needs some work." I walk up to the horses and notice that they are both covered in hay. "Well since I don't have anything else to do." I go back and grab a brush from the tack room and come back to start brushing the studs. "Nice boy." I move to the first one who just lets me brush him. "Nice boy." I talk to him as I move around him.

Once I'm done with him I move to the next one. "Good boy." I let him get my scent but he shies away. "Well come on." After a couple minutes of fighting him he finally lets me go about brushing him.

"I'm headin' in to the pisser, meet ya at the barn chica." I stop brushing and move to put the brush away after hearing a voice.

The barn door is almost shut and the only light is the natural light coming from outside. I start to move toward the door to see who's here.

"What the hell?" I hear a different voice making me stop in my tracks, what a voice it is. "Shall we see who is poking their nose around here girl?" The voice says a little louder, must be getting closer. Then I start to hear yipping, cute a puppy. "Whoa, down you evil girl." The lady laughs and oh boy what a laugh it is. My whole body comes to life at the sound of it.

I go to open the barn door, well it must be at the same time the lady is opening it because it opens pretty fast and smacks the lady in the face. "Fucker! God damn son-of-a-bitch!" Quickly, I move out the door and freeze. Damn. The lady is cussing up at storm sitting flat on her butt while her dog yips around my feet. "Timber will you stop!"

I take a quick second to take the lady before me in. Damn she's good lookin'. Tiny in height with a curvy body, long blonde hair pulled through the back of a hat in a ponytail.

"Jesus." I mutter out loud. That got her attention. "I'm sorry miss."

I watch as she tries to get up. "I'm fine." She starts to stumble a bit; quickly I wrap my hands around her waist. "Or not." She is so soft. The second I touched her, a jolt of electricity went through my whole body. That has never happened.

"Man, you're a tiny little thing." I hold her close to me and take in her looks; she's looking at me but doesn't seem to actually see. She's got the prettiest blue eyes I've ever seen. She smells like lavender and if I pulled her against me I bet she would fit perfectly.

With her dog barking and me stunned by her good looks I don't hear the other voice I heard come up.

"Oh...my...God!" I look up to see another lady; she's not a short as the ones in my arms and is a brunette.

The angel in my arms seems to get her eye sight back and slowly looks up my body. I see her fidget when she reaches my chest and then suck in a breath when she gets to my eyes. I smile down at her. She likes what she sees. I'm sure enjoying what I see.

"Cade..." She whispers, just enough for me to hear.

"Have we met, Sugar?" *Sugar? Yeah that fits this sexy little thing who I want to eat up.*

"You got to be fuckin' shittin' me!" The brunette yells as she moves toward us. *What a mouth.*

I let out a laugh and feel her fidget again and the electricity going from her body to mine goes up. "What are you doing here?" As she steps back away from me.

Damn, I want her back in my arms. I take off my hat and run a hand through my hair. "Well I use to live here Sugar. You, Tucker Price's wife or something?" I pull my hat back on a little lower this time.

She raises a brow at me and puts those little hands on her sexy hips. "I am NOT Tucker Price's wife. If that dumbass would pull his head out of his ass he has an amazing girl waiting for him at Martha's Diner in town." Damn she's ever sexier with the attitude. But with what she said I wonder how she knows the Price family then and what is going on with my best bud.

Now the brunette is next to us. "You got to be fuckin' shittin' me." She crosses her arms and glares up at me.

What a minute, I know these looks. I look back and forth at the two of them. "Runt?" I ask the brunette. Then that means. I look at the sexy little blond, no fucking way. "Monster?" I shake my head. "No way." *They grew up! And got hot!*

Runt, aka Libby laughs. "Yep it's us shithead!" She's developed quite the mouth, this I am not surprised. She moves pass me and toward the barn leaving me with grown up sexy Monster aka Emma.

Emma shakes her head and starts to follow Libby. She stops next to me and whispers. "I'm not monster anymore." *Damn straight about that!* She's grown and not a monster at all but a sexier woman that now is driving my dick crazy. Yeah, nothing can happen she's my best friend's little sister. I shake my head and follow them, stopping myself at the barn door.

"What the ..."

"I groomed them." They both turn and look at me. "I was waiting for someone to show up." I shrug and move toward them.

They turn back to the two horses. "Hey, boy." Emma calms the second one, the one that wouldn't calm at first for me. He seems fine with her.

"Hard to believe it's been ten years right monster?" *Keep it cool Masters.* I lean against the stall gate and watch her move. My dick jumps again as I take in her perfectly round ass.

"Yeah, I guess." She seems pissed by my comment. *Damn it!* She turns her attention to saddling the horse and to Libby. "Lib, how's your jaw today?" *What happened to her jaw? Is she ignoring me?*

My Cowboy

"No better than your hand." *What the hell!* "A little sore." I notice her grinning. "But probably not as bad as Lilly feels."

Lilly? Lilly who? Wait... "What did you two do to Lilly Widiner?" I glare at the both of them.

"Why would you care?" Emma asks as she mounts her horse. "She pissed me off, so I knocked her out." Libby clears her throat. "With Libby's help."

I glare up at her; Lilly Widiner was always a sweet little girl. "She's a whore now, Cade." Libby answers my thoughts. "A lot has changed since you were last here. Especially, Emma." *Yeah, no shit especially Emma!*

Emma looks at me with a bittersweet smile. "Head to my grandma's in town." She moves out the door. "That's where you will find everyone."

Then they are gone and I'm standing there with a hard dick. "Fuck." I hiss, throwing my head back. Why did she have to grow up and be so sexy? "Why does this shit happen to me?" I groan as I make my way to my truck. This fucking sucks, now I'll be fantasizing about my best friend's little sister...who probably doesn't see me in any other way that her brother's friend.

"Fuck!"

Acknowledgements

First off I need to thank my parents for allowing and giving me an amazing childhood that lead me to develop my imagination. Without your encouragement and love I wouldn't have the mind I have now. Thank you mom for listening to me talk hours on end about how I was writing My Cowboy and contributing ideas to it. (Cade's proposal)

Next, I thank my hubby for putting up with listening to me and my writing at all hours of the day and night. Without your help I wouldn't have gotten it done when I wanted to. And without your love as inspiration My Cowboy wouldn't have been possible.

To my pups, thank you for allowing mommy the time to write even when I pushed it when you needed me to get something for you. I hope you two grow strong and never give up on your hopes and dreams. I'm proving it to you now, I've always wanted to write and publish my work and I'm making my own dream come true. Don't sit around and wait, go out and take life by the horns.

Bethany and Shyda; thank you for doing the beta-reading for me. Thank you for finding some errors that I completely missed and helped them make sense.

Thank you, Jenny at Editing4Indies, you did an amazing job editing and were super helpful making everything sound and look better. Also, thank you for getting me through the editing process. You are an amazing lady!

Thank you, Ramona Lockwood for a beautiful cover. It is a perfect fit to my story. I look forward to working with you on my next cover!

To all my friends and family that have supported me in my endeavor to make my dreams come true. Thank you for your love and support.

To all the readers, thank you! Even though I did this for myself, to make my dream come true, my book would mean nothing without you buying and reading it. I hope you enjoy it as much as I did writing it. Some things I've written may not make since due to the Wyoming-ness of it but I hope you enjoy it just the same. Thank you!

If you enjoyed Emma and Cade's story, please feel free to leave a review on the website is was purchased from. Thank you so very much!

About the Author

Born and raised in Northern Wyoming. Brooke spent a great deal of her childhood and even well into her adulthood in her imagination and creating different stories. With an overactive imagination life has been truly entertaining.

A mother of two wild and reckless boys and a wife; Brooke keeps busy year round doing things with her pups and family. When she isn't writing, can usually be spotted walking somewhere in town, at the library with her youngest, or up in the mountains four-wheeling, hiking, fishing, and some hunting. A notebook and camera are never far from her side when she is out on her adventures with her family.

She loves hearing from readers and anyone who feels like talking. Feel free to pay her a visit whenever.

Sign up for Brooke's mailing list for information on new releases at:

http://www.authorbrookemay.com/newsletter.html

Stalk Brooke:

https://www.facebook.com/authorbrookemay

http://www.twitter.com/B_May88

http://instagram.com/brookemay_author

https://www.pinterest.com/authorbrookemay/

Books by Brooke

My Cowboy Series:
My Cowboy
Faith in My Cowboy
Loved by My Cowboy
My Cowgirl
She's No Cowgirl
My Bronc Riding Cowgirl
The Predator Series:
The Predator Part One
The Predator Part Two
Wildfire Knockout: A Predator Novella
Back in the Ring
Moto X Series:
Rutted (Free Prequel)
Roosted
Cased
Pinned
Bottomed Out
Squid
Powder River Pack:
A Second Chance
Call of the Alpha
It Just Comes Natural
Heartstrings Series:
Aiko
Faida

My Cowboy

Code of Honor Series:
Courage of Us
Love, Mercy
Taking Flight
Long Claw Pride:
The Mating Call
Standalones:
Scorching Hot Mess
Rogue Enforcers:
Briar
Blakely
Destination Romance:
German Wanderlust

Printed in Great Britain
by Amazon